CEREMONY OF INNOCENCE

Dorothy Cummings McLean

Ceremony of Innocence

IGNATIUS PRESS   SAN FRANCISCO

Photograph of Frankfurt am Main Hauptbahnhof courtesy of Johannes Waller
Silhouette of woman © iStockphoto.com

Other photographic elements and cover design by John Herreid

© 2013 by Ignatius Press, San Francisco
ISBN 978-1-58617-731-7
Library of Congress Control Number 2012942820
Printed in the United States of America ∞

For Mum, Dad, and Mark

Innocence always calls mutely for protection when we would be so much wiser to guard ourselves against it: innocence is like a dumb leper who has lost his bell, wandering the world, meaning no harm.

—Graham Greene
The Quiet American

Germany, 2008

PART ONE

Chapter 1

I knew he was in the flat as soon as I opened the street door. Perhaps some slight smell of him—his hair gel or his aftershave—slipped over sensual awareness straight into judgment. The veins in my wrists began to throb, and when I reached the top of the stairwell, I was breathing heavily. The door was unlocked. I went in.

"Dennis?"

His voice came from the sitting room.

"*Ja. Ich bin hier.*"

The long, narrow hallway was still lined with our books, the wall red between the volumes, between the shelves. I took my shoes off and walked into the sitting room. Dennis was in his old chair. The remote was balanced on one leather arm. A half-empty beer bottle sat on the floor. Dennis sat up very straight like a child who has been reprimanded in class. I cleared my throat.

"*Suchst du dein Handy?*"

I had imagined this moment for two weeks, and that, after all my planning, was my opening line. *Are you looking for your mobile phone?* But there he was, just as I had dreamed, dark-haired, blue-eyed, and beautiful. Strangers, both men and women, had looked at him with interest in the street and then glanced at me, gaunt and green-eyed, suddenly puzzled.

Dennis took the clothes that I gave him, but he had forgotten a number of useful objects: his phone, his diary, his grandfather's watch. Oddly, he had taken the photograph of us he liked so much. It was taken in Toronto. We're pretending to hold up the CN Tower.

"Oh, is it here?" asked Dennis in German. A drop of sweat rolled down his face. It was a hot night, and he was also nervous. "I thought maybe I had left it at Michael's place. He's in Greece."

"I know."

"I took a beer", he said meekly. "I hope you don't mind."

"No. I don't mind."

"*Tja*", said Dennis. He sat up even straighter. His words came out in a rush. "I'm looking for Suzy. Did you see her?"

"Is that why you are here? Looking for Suzy?"

Dennis said nothing.

"Now *I* need a beer."

I dropped my bag on the striped chair and walked down the hallway to the kitchen. Dennis followed me as far as the doorway. I could feel his eyes on me as I opened the refrigerator and took out a bottle.

"She said she was going to meet you near the Old Bridge."

"She told me that, too, but she didn't. Fortunately, there were some guys from work there. George. Paul Vogel. And the new guy for Reuters."

"We were supposed to meet Kurt and Markus at King Kamehameha at ten thirty."

I glanced at the kitchen clock. "Well, it's only eleven o'clock now", I said. "She's probably there."

"No, I called Kurt from Konstablerwache. She's not there."

"Well, I can't help you, Dennis. I haven't seen her."

The utensil drawer was stuck again. I pulled it open with violence and rummaged around for a bottle opener. Dennis took out his keychain and silently offered his. Then I remembered that I had given up beer.

"Never mind", I said. "I'd rather have water. It's as hot as hell in here."

"It's cooler than outside", said Dennis. Another drop of sweat coursed over his face. His blue T-shirt, with the motto "Bornheim Babe" stamped across it, stuck to his chest. We had seen it in a window and laughed. The next day I bought it for him.

"It is not in a good neighbourhood, Hanauer Landstrasse", he said now.

"Whatever", I said. "She's a big girl. Anyway, if she's not there, she's probably ditched you for something important, like a big peacenik protest at the air base."

Sarcasm rarely worked on Dennis. "But it's on Saturday, he said."

"Then maybe she's at a meeting. Either way, I couldn't care less."

"You don't understand", said Dennis. "She doesn't know Frankfurt very well. She could get lost. You know her German isn't great. And she's not strong like you. She admires you, by the way."

"That's nice."

"She says you're one of the smartest, coolest women she's ever met."

"Fantastic."

"I don't know why she didn't come home."

"Is that your home?"

"Really, I cannot think where she *could* be."

"Look, Dennis, don't worry about it. She's often late. She'll call me, or she'll call Kurt."

Dennis sat down at the wooden table. He still sat unnaturally stiffly, his posture unnaturally straight. Suzy had laughed at his way of lounging about wherever he sat, like a beauty queen, she said. She said it was unmanly. Now his hair was cut shorter than usual, and his earring was gone. Presumably he had been allowing Suzy to make a man out of him.

"It is so industrial", said Dennis. "It is not safe there. They found a Turkish girl dead in Ostend, did you know?"

"An honour killing. Her brothers did it, the papers said."

"All the same, it's a bad area."

"She has her mobile", I said.

"That's true. And she didn't call you? Maybe you should check your messages."

Despite myself, I was touched by his simple faith that I wouldn't shout or scream or tell him to go to hell. Obediently, I went to the sitting room and took my mobile from my bag. Dennis followed me in and retrieved his beer. I checked my messages. Nothing new.

"I'm sorry, Dennis", I said. "Nothing."

The intercom buzzed, and Dennis relaxed.

"There", I said. "That will be her."

I pressed the button to let her in. But the heavy tread on the stairs was not hers, nor was the lighter tread that followed. There was a staccato German rap on the door. I opened it and saw two plain-clothes policemen, one young, one middle-aged. They were both sweating.

"Frau McClelland?"

"Yes, certainly. Can I help you?"

The young cop looked solemnly at me while behind him the middle-aged cop looked over my head at the hallway. "There's been an incident. Do you mind if we come in?"

I said, "An incident? My family? Were you sent by British police?"

"British? *Also*. No, Frau McClelland. Not your family."

Both cops stepped into the hallway, shrinking it. I gestured them into the sitting room, but only the middle-aged one went in. The younger one kept his eyes on my face. "I am sorry to say that there has been an incident involving one of your friends, Frau McClelland. We would like you to come with us to the police station."

"What happened?"

"If you would come with us to the police station, it will all be explained."

The older cop was looming over Dennis, asking for his papers. Dennis, alarmed but obedient, was taking them out of his wallet. The cop read them aloud, lingering on his Christian name. "Deniz Erlichmann. Turkish?"

"My mother's father was Turkish. Everyone calls me Dennis, actually."

"*Klar*. We'd appreciate it if you came too."

"Yes, okay." Out of habit, perhaps, Dennis looked at me for confirmation. I nodded.

We sat silently in the back of the green police car. I looked out at the brightly lit street, its bars bright and peopled beside shuttered cafés, stores, and bakeries. Dennis looked straight ahead. After a little while, he fiddled in his trouser pocket—white cargo capris, I never liked them—and took out his MP3 player. He fit the earplugs into his ears and disappeared inside himself.

It was not a long journey. We got out at the police station and followed the cops into the sterile building. We were left to ourselves in a waiting room after being offered coffee. Dennis took the plugs out of his ears.

"What do you think it is?" he asked.

"It's probably something to do with Peace Now."

"Peace Now? But we haven't done anything wrong!"

"Trespassing is wrong; maybe conspiring to trespass is wrong, too. Peace Now is a pest. The police don't like pests."

The stubborn look I know so well passed over Dennis' face. It made him look heroic instead of pigheaded. It wrung my heart, seeing it again after two weeks' absence.

"I won't tell them anything", he said.

"Wait and see what they ask first."

A policewoman called my name, and I was shown into an office. The Kommissar, whom I knew from church, was standing in the doorway, burly, balding, and red-faced. I stuck my hand out. He shook it heartily. We might have been at Mass.

"Ah, Frau McClelland. I'm very glad you came. Coffee?"

"It's too late at night, thanks."

"Will you take *Apfelchorle*?"

"Thank you. I will."

Herr Krause went out and came back in again with a bottle of apple fizz and two glasses. He shut the door, and I thought of the old interrogation chairs of East Germany with removable cloth for catching and analysing sweat.

"*Tja*", said Herr Krause. "I am sorry to ask you to come down here, but as a matter of fact, I am hoping that you will answer a few questions."

"I would be happy to", I said. "How can I help you?"

In answer, Herr Krause opened a folder on his desk and pushed a photograph at me. It was a black-and-white shot of Suzy, her hair wrapped in a mottled bandana. She was grinning, with her mouth open.

"Suzy Davis", I said. "She's a language student. A Canadian."

"Do you know her well?"

"Not very well. She's more than ten years younger than me. You could say I know her on a superficial level."

Herr Krause picked up the photograph and looked at it before shutting it back in its folder. "Tell me how you met her."

I explained that it had been Suzy who had met me, that night in the King Kamehameha, in the lady's room, as a matter of fact, desirous of a tampon and not knowing the word in German. She had had some bad conversational luck by the time I came along, and although she appeared cheerful when she trotted out "*Sprechen Sie English?*" for my benefit, there was a note of desperation in her voice. Her relief when I answered her in English was almost comic. For a Canadian abroad, she was very noisy.

"You are yourself a Canadian, are you not?" asked Krause, and I was startled. I always travel on my British passport and renew my Canadian document only to appease my mother's fears that if I don't keep renewing it, it will be harder to get. I wondered what else Krause knew about me, and whether there was a file about me on that desk or sitting concealed in a drawer.

"I was born there. I grew up in Scotland."

"You speak German with almost no accent", said Krause.

I smiled and remained silent.

"But then, of course, it helps to live with a native German", he continued. "I take it that you and your boyfriend are still living together."

"As a matter of fact," I said stiffly, "we are on a break. A lover's quarrel. Dennis is staying with friends. With Suzy, actually. But I suppose you know that if—"

"If?"

"If you're investigating Suzy. Look, Herr Krause, what is this about? If it's Suzy's silly peace group, I assure you I am not a member. Neither is Dennis, except tangentially. I write only about religious groups, Pax Christi and so forth. I have no interest in Peace Now. They're half-baked Marxists, or something. They wear Palestinian scarves and Che Guevara T-shirts. Kid's stuff."

"You yourself are not political, then?"

"Certainly not. My employer leans to the right, I suppose, but it's a Catholic media group. Socially conservative and politically liberal. Liberal, as Americans understand it anyway. I just go with whatever the Church says."

"But not always."

I saw that he was thinking of Dennis, who sometimes showed up at Mass, and of my most interesting habit of not receiving Communion. Catholics eventually notice when other Catholics don't. In Scotland, it's rude to notice. Germany isn't Scotland.

"No, not always."

Krause fiddled with his papers. "You're divorced, I find. Have you not thought of applying for an annulment?"

"I haven't had to. My husband began the process last spring."

"So this means you could marry again in the Church?"

"I presume so, but I don't know what this has to do with Suzy Davis."

"Suzy Davis is dead", said Herr Krause. "We pulled her out of the Main River an hour ago."

I sat there silently. *Whatever he says*, I told myself, *I am innocent.*

"Is this surprising news?"

"Yes and no. I am sorry. I need a minute. She was very young."

"Twenty-two."

"Exactly." My voice shook. My mind stood a little apart, listening to my voice shake and feeling tears fill my eyes. It often does that when I have something to hide. I was wary but pleased by my reaction.

"Why is it not surprising?"

"Suzy knew a lot of dodgy people. Not just university students. Adults. Adults happy to exploit the enthusiasm and the naïveté of the young."

"Just so. Do you know who they were?"

"I'm sorry, no. I kept right away from that crowd. They thought I was a reactionary anyway, being religious."

"And Dennis?"

"He's religious, too. His great-uncle is the Cardinal Archbishop of Kleinburg. But he might know who the adults are. He knows Suzy's friends better than I do."

"Did you like Suzy, Frau McClelland?"

"Yes, I did. That is, I liked her up until Dennis left me. Then I hated her."

"That's very frank. Thank you. And now?"

"And now I am sorry for her. She loved life, and singing, and dancing, and making jokes. She was very young. And in some ways stupid, in the way the young are stupid. And moral, as she understood the concept."

"Moral?"

"She was a vegetarian. She cared about animals. And Palestinian children, battered wives, endangered whales, and all that. She didn't drink or drug or sleep around. Do you want to know where I was tonight?"

"I do."

"I was supposed to meet Suzy at Il Gattopardo, by the Old Bridge. She wanted to talk, woman to woman, assuage her conscience, make sure we could all be friends. It's not far from my office on the Kaiserstrasse. I went there with George Santos, the AP man. He was meeting Simon Reinhardt from the *Frankfurter Allgemeine* and some other journalists for drinks. Paul Vogel was there and Petra Schattschneider. Suzy was supposed to meet me at nine. She didn't. That didn't surprise me; she's usually late. I called her at nine thirty, and she didn't answer her mobile. At ten or so, I called again, and when there was no answer, I went for a walk over the Old Bridge. She lives in Sachsenhausen; I thought I might meet her on the way. But I didn't, so I got on the S-Bahn at the Südbahnhof."

"You didn't go to her flat."

"No. I didn't want to see Dennis."

Herr Krause sighed, and he got to his feet. "Would you mind identifying her? I'm sorry to ask you to do this, but we haven't been able to locate any family, and you're the first of her friends to come in."

"Does she look very bad?" I asked. "I'm sorry, I don't want to be cowardly. Was she shot, or strangled, or what?"

I had a horror film vision of Suzy blue in the face, eyes wide, tongue protruding.

"So far as we can tell, she was forcibly drowned", said Krause, regretfully. "Please follow me."

I followed him down a corridor and down a stairwell. He pushed open a door to what looked like an operating room. There were two masked women—forensics officers, I think they are called—bustling around a figure on a table, mostly covered by a sheet.

"Excuse me", said Krause. "You permit?"

"Yes, certainly", said the one nearest the door. She stood aside.

"Do you recognise her?" asked Krause.

"Yes", I said. "Certainly."

She looked even more vulnerable, more alien there on that table. Younger, more foreign, the stud in her nose more pronounced, her dyed blue hair more blue. Why couldn't she have just stayed in Toronto? I wondered. Worked in a clothing shop on trendy Queen Street West. Spent the long weekends in Montreal with some McGill student she hooked up with. Applied to do a master's degree in peace studies or world religions. Stayed far away from Europe.

"Do you know where we might reach her family?"

"I'm sorry. All I know is that they live near Toronto. She didn't get along with them. You'll have to ask Dennis. Can I go home now? Suddenly, I feel very tired."

Dennis was waiting for me on the bench. His face was red. He had been crying. He was crying still, tears trickling slowly down his handsome face. He looked up when I approached and almost before I could register it, he stood, pulled me into his arms, and buried his face in my caramel-dyed hair.

"I'm sorry", he said. "I am so sorry."

"There, there", I said in English. "Oh dear, *Deniz*, oh dear. Don't take on so. There's nothing we can do."

And as I held him, I could feel his heart beating against my face, and with every beat, I thought *mine, not hers, mine.*

Dennis pulled away and dabbed at his eyes with the back of his hand. He gave a half-laugh. "Only you and my grandmother call me *Deniz*."

"Oh, aye. *Alten Damen zusammen*."

"I feel cold", he said. His teeth were chattering.

"Sit down", I said. "It's probably shock. I'll tell them to get us a cab."

"No, I want to walk. Or we can take the U-Bahn. I don't know. I want to go home."

"To Sachsenhausen or your parents' place?"

"I mean home with you", said Dennis. "Here in Bornheim. May I, please?"

"Of course you can."

"She looked so dead", he said. "I have never seen a dead person before. Not for real."

"So you identified her?"

"I had to. They said there was no one else to do it."

We walked. The night had grown cooler at last. The cafés and bars still rang with music and the noise of television sets. Dennis ducked down a side street, away from the lights and the people. I followed. Bornheim was mostly spared by the bombs in the war; the houses are lovely. The trees are old.

After a long silence, Dennis began to chatter. The interviewer had asked him his movements. Where had he spent the evening? Who had seen him? Thank God, Marcus had come over for drinks. Marcus would tell them. And he and Marcus had both spoken to Michael in Greece over the computer. There must be a record of that on the computer. Suzy had Skype. I should have Skype, too. It was great; it was a way around the terrible mobile fees, although not as convenient. I let him chatter himself out. There was a police car following us; I chose not to mention it.

Our street was empty. The building includes a daycare centre in the front, ground-floor flat. In the afternoons, the children go out to play, and when I am home, I like to listen to their laughter and their amusing observations and negotiations. The playground toys looked ghostly, colours washed out in the dark. The scent of the late roses was heavy in the air. Dennis opened the gate, and I slipped through ahead of him. I unlocked the door, and he followed me upstairs. Without saying anything, he took off his shoes and went straight into the bedroom.

19

I went into the back sitting room and rolled up the rug. I found my hiding place and lifted off the wooden tile. Underneath was Dennis' stash of weed.

Dennis had not remained in the bedroom for long. He was rummaging around in the kitchen. I stood in the doorway and watched.

"I need something to eat", he said. "Are you hungry?"

"Maybe later. Do you want to smoke?"

"*Also*", said Dennis. "I forgot that was here."

"Then come into the bedroom. If you pass out, I won't be able to pick you up."

That night I woke up with Dennis' arms around me, and his breath in my hair. It might have been four months ago, before Suzy arrived in Frankfurt. We were back where we left off, Dennis and I. Well, not exactly. Not exactly.

Poor bloody Suzy.

Chapter 2

The evening Suzy spoke to me in the ladies' room of the King
Kamehameha, I had seen quite enough of student activists, German
and foreign. I thought the German students were particularly funny,
with their outrage over increases to their nominal tuition fees, but
the Canadians were the worst. Anti-Americanism was the shared creed
of all the student activists, but the Canadians made themselves the
supreme pontiffs. No American fellow traveller could be abjectly self-
hating enough for a Canadian; she always found a place to stick the
knife in.

But Suzy wasn't like that. When I asked her if she were an American, her grin didn't falter. "Close enough! I'm Canadian."

"No way", I said. "After a statement like that, I want to see your
passport."

"What?"

"Canadians don't like Americans."

"Oh well, that's just the foreign policy. I have millions of American
friends."

She disappeared into a stall with my spare tampon. "What about
you? Are you British?"

"Close enough. I'm Canadian."

"Shut up! I'm serious."

"I am serious. I was born in Toronto, but I migrated to Scotland."

"Random", said Suzy. "That's, like, totally backward."

She emerged from her stall. She was a colourful figure, was Suzy.
That night she was wearing a short pink wig, a silver top, and pink,
flared trousers of some clingy fabric. The stud in her nose was red.
She had a whole collection of nasal adornments, I was later to discover: studs, rings, chains. But on her it was never scary; it was almost
comic.

"You saved my life!" she announced. "I should buy you a drink!"

"Now I really do want to see your passport."

"Why?"

"Drinks here are expensive. Canadians are notoriously cheap."

"Shut up! Here, look!" She pulled the blue document, much more battered than my own, from her silver knapsack and handed it to me. I flipped it open, and sure enough, Suzy Davis was born in Scarborough, Canada, ten days before Dennis was born in Bonn.

I made a face to tease her. "Scarborough? Ugh."

"Oh yeah? Then where were you born?"

"Toronto."

"Prove it."

"What?"

"I showed you mine; now you show me yours."

"Bloody cheek! I don't have mine with me."

"Ha!" said Suzy. "I bet you're full of it. Come and meet the posse."

"The what?"

"The posse. My entourage. Two of them are Canadians, too."

I thought of Dennis. He was waiting at a table with Marcus and Michael. Normally, I didn't like leaving him alone at the King Kamehameha. It's expensive and trendy, and I didn't like the way the international party set gravitated toward him. But it was still early, not even midnight, so I accepted Suzy's invitation.

Her friends, three young men and a bored-looking girl, were standing by one of the floodlit bars over the dance floor. To my surprise, two of them were German. It is unusual for tourists to have German friends; usually they keep to themselves.

It was easy to tell the North Americans from the Germans; the Germans were better dressed. The two Canadian men were wearing jeans and hoodies; they were drinking beer. The other man was German; his hair was carefully mussed and gelled into place. The collar of his polo shirt was turned up. He was cautiously sipping at a cocktail in a wide martini glass. The bored-looking girl was wearing fashionable specs and a dress I recognised from the window of an expensive shop on Goethestrasse. She too was drinking a cocktail.

"Hey, guys", shouted Suzy, pulling me by my arm. "This girl saved my life. And you'll never guess where she's from. I'm sorry, I totally don't know your name. What's your name?"

I told them my name. There was handshaking all around. The Canadians were Sean and Mike; the Germans were Lukas and Julia.

Suzy almost shivered with excitement as she implored her friends to guess where I was born. They all guessed wrongly. When I confessed the answer, both Canadian men looked deeply suspicious. "From where?"

"Toronto."

"Oh, yeah? So what's the name of the hockey team?"

"The Maple Leafs."

"And where do they play?"

"Maple Leaf Gardens."

Sean made a rude, harsh sound. "Sorry, try again. The Air Canada Centre."

I had spoken without thinking. Actually, I had seen the new place the summer previously while visiting my grandparents.

"What's the football team?"

"Oh, leave her alone", interrupted Suzy. "Who cares?"

Lukas listened to this solemnly and asked a few questions about ice hockey. Like most young Germans, his English was excellent, if idiosyncratic.

"I do not see how Canadians are different from Americans in that respect", said the bored girl, Julia. "You are both obsessed with sport."

Sean turned beet red, but Mike chuckled.

"Everybody's obsessed with sport", he said.

Julia stared at him, frowning. "I am sorry, but that is not true. And your sports, American football and ice hockey, they are very violent, I find. They are obviously a channel for warlike aggression."

"Get real", said Sean. "We don't have warlike aggression. We're peacekeepers, like I told you."

"But that is not true. You have troops in Afghanistan."

"Yeah, but that's only because there is a conservative government in power. Ordinary Canadians don't want soldiers there. Just the right-wing warmongers."

"And they are in Iraq, too, of course."

"That's a lie", shouted Sean. "We don't have any soldiers in Iraq. We told the Yanks to screw themselves."

"But she's got a good point", said Suzy. "It's all part of the so-called War against Terror. And if Harper had been in power when it started, we *would* be in Iraq."

I could see where this was going, and I felt fatigue setting in. By nature, I am a morning person. To survive long nights in clubs without

23

losing my temper, I had to stay on the dance floor or get drunk or high. My boredom threshold was low.

"Well", I said. "It was very nice to meet you all, but I had better go back to my friends."

"Wait", said Suzy and clung to my arm. "I totally want to buy you a drink!"

"Thanks. Maybe another time."

"You sure?" Suzy made a tragic, baby face.

"Sorry. You drink it for me."

"But I don't drink", wailed Suzy. "You sure? Just one little, eeny, weeny, tiny, drink?"

"No, really. Maybe next time."

"Okay", she said, pouting. "So is this, like, your crib, or what?"

"My what?"

"Your hangout, you know. Where you go to chill."

"In a manner of speaking", I said. "Are you here for long or—?"

"Oh yeah", said Suzy happily. "I'm totally hanging out."

She flashed me a peace sign, and then cupped her hand into a C. "See ya!"

She was young, so very young. Idealistic, friendly, gullible. Perhaps I should have paid more attention when she decried the "War on Terror". Perhaps I could have pointed out that the world was not that simple, not divided between warmongers and peacekeepers, soldiers and civilians. But as it turned out, she didn't really make those distinctions herself.

Suzy and all those men. Julia wasn't particularly girlish. Suzy was looking for a girlfriend, an older sister or a mother, a young hip mother. But I wasn't interested. I had problems of my own, problems that I could not discuss with my own old-fashioned mother. I had Dennis, and frankly, I wasn't interested in a constant reminder that I was ... not old, but older. And Suzy's idealism, her friendliness and her high spirits, rubbed against my conscience like sandpaper over a wound. So I left her liberal platitudes unchecked, and I went down the stairs and through the dance floor of swaying, twisting bodies and found Dennis and our friends sitting at our table in the enormous, twig-roofed porch.

Marcus got up, and I slid beside Dennis. He put his arm around my waist and gestured to a frosty glass of clear liquid sitting untouched on the table.

24

"I got you a G & T", he said.

There was a thirty-something woman standing at the bar across from us. She was dressed to impress, and she kept glancing at our table. I ran my hand up Dennis' back.

"Mmm", he said. "What's that for?"

"And what have you all been talking about?" I asked.

Marcus leaned over, his eyes twinkling behind his glasses. "We have been discussing the best kind of democracy."

"Oh, for the love of heaven", I said.

I looked up at the ceiling and saw stars twinkling through the branches. They swam a little, perhaps because of the G & T.

"What do you think, Cat?" asked Dennis. "What is the best form of democracy?

"To hell with politics", I said. "Which one of you boys is going to dance with me?"

* * *

I woke up, as always, at 7:00 AM Now that my leg was better, I could go to my gym again. When I returned, Dennis was still asleep. It might have been two months ago. I took a shower and dried my hair with a towel; I never used a hairdryer before Dennis moved in, and his was now at Suzy's. I ground espresso beans, and Dennis emerged from the bedroom. He sat huddled at the table wrapped in the duvet, a victim of bedhead.

"*Tag*", he said.

I gave him a long espresso and turned back to the machine. Neither of us mentioned Suzy.

"Do you have class today?" I asked.

"At eleven. But I have to get my books."

"I'll drive you."

The door of Suzy's postmodern building was open, and there were two police cars in front. On the front lawn, an inspector was taking a statement from a red-faced blonde woman. He wouldn't let Dennis in, but I flashed him my press pass, and he reluctantly gestured me inside. The elevator was out of service. I climbed the clever, windowed staircase to the fifth floor. The door to Suzy's flat was wide open. I walked in to find it full of men in plastic suits and gloves. My fellow parishioner Krause was standing in the sunlit living-room window, gazing down at the street.

25

He turned. He was holding a large green book in his hand. "Ah, Frau McClelland. Good morning."

"Good morning." I hesitated.

"Please come in", he said. "We're almost done here."

"I've come for Dennis' things. His books. He has a class at eleven."

Herr Krause tapped the book thoughtfully. "Do you know what this is?"

From where I stood I could read the script on the spine, but I shook my head.

"It's the Koran in English and Arabic", said Krause. "Unusual, isn't it?"

"Perhaps", I said. "Suzy was interested in world religions. She felt strongly about Palestine."

We looked at the mantelpiece over the disused fireplace. Between two bronze elephants, Suzy had amassed a number of volumes by Naomi Klein, Karen Armstrong, Noam Chomsky. I wondered if she had brought them with her or found them in a local English bookstore.

"She seems to have had an affinity for the East", said Krause. "This décor."

The flat was richly appointed with bright cushions embroidered in gold. Sari fabrics, not as common in Frankfurt as in Toronto, hung from the windows and the walls. Persian miniatures, cut from art books, hung in little gilt frames.

"Very lavish for a student", Krause remarked. "Are her parents rich?"

I thought of Suzy's amicably divorced parents, both of them civil servants, she had said.

"Suzy was very independent", I said. "I don't think she would take money from her parents unless she was in trouble."

"Interesting", said the detective. "Did Herr Erlichmann pay for this, do you think?"

"Dennis doesn't have a feather to fly with. He has a part-time job in a bookstore, of course, and his parents make him an allowance. But he has to show them an itemised list of all expenses."

"I'm sorry to ask you this, but did either of them receive money from you?"

"I closed our joint account when Dennis left our flat. I've stood Suzy drinks. That's all."

"Thank you. I am sorry to ask such personal questions, but it is my job, you understand."

"Quite."

We moved into the bedroom and located Dennis' suitcase under the bed. His backpack was sitting in a corner; the books inside were very neatly arranged, having no doubt been searched. I found his other books on Suzy's desk and put them in the suitcase. Krause watched as I opened the double closet and pulled Dennis' clothes from the hangers and the drawers. The bedroom continued Suzy's Arabian Nights theme; there was even a decent imitation Persian carpet on the floor. The bathroom, which was newly tiled, was workaday German, cluttered by Dennis' dozen bottles of hair products and shaving kit. His hairdryer hung from a hook. I took it down and put the bottles and kit into a plastic bag while Krause watched from the doorway.

My eye fell upon a black enamelled box. I carefully took the lid off; Suzy's nose jewellery glittered inside.

"This is Suzy's", I said. "I'd like to keep it, if I may. After all, she was my friend—of a kind."

"I'm afraid that is not possible", said Krause.

"Just one of the nose rings, then", I said. "The red one, maybe. You pick."

Krause picked up the box and looked inside.

"I always wonder what they do when they have a cold", he said. "One ring then. We will say nothing more of this."

"Thanks", I said and took out the ruby red one I had first noticed in the ladies' room in King Kamehameha. I slipped it into my pocket.

"It is always very sad when a young girl is killed", said Krause, and I remembered that he had a daughter spending a study year abroad in New York. "It was not particularly late at night, either. I do not recollect if I asked you already, but did you see her at all that day?"

"No", I said. "She called me in the late afternoon to reconfirm our dinner appointment, and that was the last I heard from her."

"It is strange about her bicycle", said Krause. "Dennis said that she took her bicycle when she went out, but we did not find it near the crime scene."

"It was probably stolen", I said, suddenly angry. "Why does it matter? Do you expect to find mysterious gravel in the treads?"

"Perhaps", said Krause. "Frau McClelland, do you have any idea who killed Suzy Davis?"

"I don't have the faintest idea."

"But really. Any idea at all?"

"Suzy mixed herself up with some dodgy people. She was an optimist. She trusted people, even enough to hitchhike. Anyone who had any claim to victim status was a potential saint to Suzy. She made friends easily, even with Turkish shopkeepers with hardly any German and less English. She had friends who were PKK supporters, Hamas supporters, Hezbollah."

"We know all that", said Krause. "What I am looking for is a name."

"I don't know many names", I said. "When Suzy talked about her activist friends, I stopped listening. There are two Canadians, Sean and Mike, and some Germans and Americans. A Czech, I think. A couple of Swedes, and a Turkish German."

"Like Mr. Erlichmann."

"Hardly", I said. "Dennis is as German as you are, Herr Krause. His grandfather thoroughly assimilated himself. He even became a Christian before marriage."

"Is it a sore point?"

"Not for me. Dennis' sister converted to Islam. 'Reverted', she says. She calls herself a Turk. It did not go down well with the family. She rarely calls them now."

"Where does she live?" asked the detective casually.

I assumed he knew already, so I told him. We went into the bedroom, and he politely picked up Dennis' suitcase and knapsack. I preceded him down the stairs. Dennis was leaning on the car with his arms folded, earplugs planted in his ears. He was wearing his yellow-tinted sunglasses, and his eyes were bright green behind them. As he saw us coming, he pulled the plugs out and stepped forward to take his belongings from Krause.

"I'll take the luggage back to Bornheim", I said, for the Kommissar's benefit. "We can talk later."

"Thank you", said Dennis. He put the suitcase and his knapsack in the boot. "Do you have time to take me to school?"

"Yes", I said. "You drive, if you like."

I handed him the keys, and he went around the car to the driver's door. Krause looked after him.

"He's a very good-looking young man", he said.

His voice, to my sensitive ear, carried a note of irony. I bid him a curt good day and slid into the front passenger seat.

Chapter 3

The first time Suzy met Dennis was on the Zeil, Frankfurt's pedestrian shopping street. It stretches from watchtower to ancient watchtower, offering all the brand-name goods of the earth. It was late in the evening, not very warm yet. The trees were in full blossom, and their heavy scent lingered even in the concrete city centre.

Dennis and I were sitting at a table outside a café, Dennis with his first beer of the evening, and I with my first gin and tonic. Dennis didn't like gin, but he liked that I drank it. For him, it was the alcoholic distillation of Britain. Our evening plans were not firm as yet; Dennis was awaiting a call from our friend Marcus. For now, we were content to sit, Dennis reading me his English assignment, and I listening as I watched his face. Then Suzy burst into view beside our table. She paused and gave a little wave. This time she was wearing a blue wig and a blue nose stud.

"Hi", she said. "Remember me? You saved my life at the King Kamehama two weeks ago. I totally owe you a drink."

"Of course", I replied. "Dennis, this is Suzy. Suzy, this is my boyfriend, Dennis."

"I am very pleased to meet you", said Dennis in his stilted would-be Oxbridge accent. He looked swiftly at me and added in German, "Is she American?"

"Canadian. A *noisy* Canadian."

"*Toll.*"

He offered his tanned hand to Suzy. Suzy stared at him for a moment without taking his hand. When she finally realised it was there, she giggled and blushed.

"Oh my goodness, I'm totally out of it." She shook his hand, "Hi, Dennis, nice to meet you."

She sat down at the table. "If you're not doing anything, I thought maybe you would like to have a drink with me and my friends. They're really cool."

She turned around in her chair and waved vigorously at the café next to ours. To my astonishment, the cool blonde woman who waved back was Silke von Dreich. The raven-haired woman sitting with her was Countess Piroli, talking into her mobile. How in the name of heaven, I wondered, did Suzy get into that crowd?

"Have you sold out to the capitalists?" I asked.

Suzy laughed. "I never judge anybody by their parents", she said. "Take mine for example. Bor-ing! Anyway, come and have a drink. Dennis, too, of course."

Dennis looked at me. I nodded.

"We would be delighted", he said in his careful English.

We got up, and Dennis slung his knapsack over his shoulder. Anna Maria Piroli closed her tiny, crystal-studded phone and hid it in her Gucci bag. Her eyes were bright, and I wondered if she was coked up yet. She was naturally so hyper, it was often hard to tell.

"*Bella*", she said, and we air-kissed. Silke half-stood, and we repeated the gesture, one foreign to us both but now unfortunately one of the indisputable rituals of polite society. I could smell whisky on her breath.

"And the little Dennis", said Anna Maria in English. "So cute."

She held out her hand mockingly, and Dennis kissed it with aplomb.

"I am surprised to see you", said Silke. "I thought you would be in Berlin, covering the anti-Pope protests."

"I am surprised to see you", I said. "I thought you'd be in Milan, covering the shows."

"In May? Milan is dead."

"And Frankfurt is alive?"

"Frankfurt is heaven", said Anna Maria. "Simply heaven."

"Frankfurt is crap", said Silke sourly. "But my mother is in hospital."

"So you already know each other?" asked Suzy. "I thought Catriona was my discovery."

"Darling," said Anna Maria, "how silly. Everybody knows Catriona. She is the most famous British journalist in Germany."

"Hardly", I said.

"And her little book, so clever! I haven't read it, but Florian says it is a work of genius."

"Really?" Suzy's eyes were huge. "What is it about?"

Dennis laughed. "She will not tell you. She never discusses her writing. Not even with me."

"I never discuss my writing. Writers never discuss writing. We discuss sales."

"*Genau*", said Silke. "I will drink to that. Where the hell is that waiter?"

I ordered my second gin and tonic of the evening, and Dennis requested his second beer. Once again, I wondered what on earth Suzy was doing with the butterfly set. As if reading my thoughts, she burst into speech.

"Silke is writing a story on my peace group", said Suzy happily. "It's really cool."

"It's part of something I'm doing on Palestine", said Silke. "The increase of student groups who support Palestinian sovereignty. Student networking across the world. Peace Now is a perfect example."

"It's great that such a big magazine is taking notice", said Suzy. "That's just great. I mean, German *Vogue!*"

"No surprise there", I said. "Palestine is still a fashion must-have. Not even Darfur has the same chic."

Silke didn't like my tone. "Do you mean that you support Israel?"

"Me? I'm completely apolitical."

"But you write for the Catholic Church. Doesn't the Church think what the Jews have been doing to the Palestinians is sinful?"

"The Israelis."

"That's what I said", snapped Silke.

"You said 'the Jews'."

The word hung quivering in the air for a moment before Anna Maria knocked it away. "Politics, politics. Boring! I want to talk about sex. Dennis, tell me, I am dying to know, have you ever been with two women at once?"

Dennis choked on his beer, coughed, and spluttered. Silke patted him on the back.

"Anna Maria", yelped Suzy. She too had turned pink.

"It is a natural question to ask. Dennis, you are such a beautiful boy. When I first saw you that night in that club, the one with the funny name, I thought that for sure you must be gay. But you are not. Aren't we lucky?"

"*I* am lucky", I said. I found Dennis' foot under the table and stepped on it gently. He put his other foot on top of mine.

"Yes, you are", said Dennis loftily, trying to look cool. His face was still flushed.

31

"I wish you would *share* him, darling", said Anna Maria.

"Sorry", I said.

"You can't keep him forever. It wouldn't be fair."

"We are getting married, by the way", said Dennis.

"*Dennis.*"

The waiter appeared with the drinks. We ignored him as he set the glasses down.

"How sweet!" shrieked Anna Maria.

"Have you set a date?" asked Silke.

"No", I said. "This is just a projection into the future."

Dennis was silent.

"Don't be in such a hurry, darling", said Anna Maria. "You have all the time in the *world.*"

"Marriage is very risky when there is such a difference in age", said Silke.

Anna Maria said, "Silke, *darling!*"

Silke shrugged. "I'm sorry. It is a statement of fact. And you are too young to marry, Dennis. You haven't even got your *Diplom* yet, have you?"

Anna Maria's phone rang, and she answered it.

Dennis scowled at me and swigged his beer.

"I don't think age matters", said Suzy. "Age ain't nothing but a number. Besides, I couldn't tell that Catriona was older."

"Catriona has very good skin", said Silke. "All the British do if they don't lie out in the sun. But you're beginning to get a wrinkle, Cat, right beside your mouth. It's never too early to begin talking to a dermatologist. Mine is very good. I'll give you his card."

"Oh my goodness!" said Suzy, shocked. "I think Cat looks great!"

"It's okay, Suzy", I said. "This is Germany. Germans say what they think—if they trust you. They don't mean to be insulting."

"Yes, naturally", said Silke. "We are not like the Americans, who smile and say nice things all the time, and then close factories or drop bombs."

Anna Maria shut her phone. "Florian says he is leaving now for the party. You must come to the party. It will be wonderful. Everybody will be there. You must come, Catriona, and bring your little Dennis. Gustav will love him, simply love and worship him. And Florian is dying to talk to you about your book. Suzy, you must come and tell everybody about your peace group. They will be impressed, don't you think, Silke?"

"No," said Silke, "but Suzy might make some very good contacts. Ahmed al-Ahmain is a good friend of Gustav's now."

"Ahmed, I adore him! So sweet! Pay for the drinks, darling, and I will call my car."

The last time I arrived at one of their parties with Dennis in a limo, we got a lot of grief from his great-uncle the Archbishop. Limousines attract photographers, and life is difficult enough. So we all walked to the taxi stand at the end of the Zeil, and Dennis and I followed Anna Maria's Cadillac by cab. Suzy had hovered by Dennis, somewhat nervously, I thought, but Anna Maria carted her off to the limousine.

It was now after midnight, and the younger crowd was heading for the U-Bahn. The streets of the Innerstadt were full of colour and light, neon and noise.

"I like Suzy", I said to Dennis. "She's very sweet."

"She is noisy," said Dennis, "but not as noisy as your Italian friend."

"Anna Maria is not really my friend", I said. "And that's probably coke."

The limo pulled up to a bronze-glass skyscraper. We got out of the cab and followed Suzy and her glamorous patrons into the building. There was a two-storey waterfall in the gold-lit marble lobby. Dennis wandered over to look at the goldfish in the pond.

"Darling Dennis, come here", carolled Anna Maria. "Come here, darling!"

The elevator shot upward fifty stories. The socialites repaired their makeup as Suzy and Dennis stared out over the river below.

"Isn't it just, like, totally gorgeous?" said Suzy to Dennis.

"Please?"

"*Schön*", I provided.

"Ah, well you see," said Dennis in his ersatz Oxbridge accent, "it isn't real, actually. No, it's all done with mirrors. It is the great secret of German engineering."

"No!"

"It's true. We're not supposed to tell foreigners, so don't tell anyone I told you."

"Maybe I'll tell the newspapers."

"The newspapers know it already, but I am afraid I will have to shoot you."

He blethered on while Suzy giggled.

She stopped giggling when we reached Gustav's flat. The door opened to a roar of techno and a throng of weaving bodies, many of them shirtless. Along the floor-to-ceiling windows, a film screen had been set up, flashing pornographic scenes from Japanese cartoons. Bodies twined on the couches, and the maple floors were littered with paper cones. Paper cones, filled to the brim with sweets and pills, spilled out of a cardboard paper cone on a centre table, a tribute to the traditional *Schültute* of German first-graders. I got one glance of Suzy's shocked face before Anna Maria pulled her away to meet somebody.

"Poor Suzy", I yelled to Dennis over the beat. "I am going to have to rescue her."

"What?"

"Rescue!"

"Catriona, look", said Dennis. "That is Rainer Hencke."

"Who?"

"The footballer. Wait here."

He squeezed my arm and weaved through the squirming bodies toward a lean young man with a shaved head. He was leaning against the wall listening to a big, beefy man in a sharp Italian suit, and looking bored. When Dennis approached, he straightened up. They shook hands.

I had my bag tucked under my arm. It buzzed against my side, and I pulled out my phone. It was Marcus. I put a finger in my ear, but I couldn't hear a word. I shouted at Marcus not to hang up and found the bathroom. A tall, redheaded, transgendered woman lurched out, still wiping her nose, and I went in, locking the door behind me. There was white powder dusted over the black marble sink.

"Where are you?" demanded Marcus. "Dennis isn't answering his phone."

"We're still in the Innerstadt. We're at a party."

"But Kurt and Michael and I are all at KK!"

"We'll be there. I'll find Dennis. Who's on the door tonight?"

"Eberhardt. Don't worry. He knows you're coming."

A blonde woman I'd seen on TV was talking to Dennis and Rainer Hencke. I wove through the jammed flat, looking for Suzy. At last, I found Anna Maria leaning against the refrigerator, making out with her blond boyfriend, Florian von Brandenburg zu Hessich. I had known him at Cambridge. He had been a nice chap, rumoured to be brilliant, before he got into cocaine. I plucked at Anna Maria's elbow.

"Where's Suzy?"

"Ah, Catriona, hallo", said Florian. "I have read your most interesting book. Would you do me the honour of having coffee with me this week? I have a few suggestions that you might find helpful."

"I'm going to Berlin", I said. "Right now I'm looking for a blue-haired Canadian girl. Where did you put her?"

"Darling. I introduced her to Ahmed. But then darling Florian came and stole me away, and I lost her."

At last, I found Suzy in the library, sitting nervously on the end of a couch while a drunken Dutchman in a tuxedo tried to interest her in a party he was planning near the Nordsee. Her face, when she saw me, was so flooded with relief, I had to smile. She struggled to her feet. Aggrieved at the loss of his audience, the drunk man seized her arm. I took a half-filled glass from an end table and threw it in his face. He let go, cursing and sputtering.

"Okay, kid", I said to Suzy. "Let's go."

I found Dennis leaning in the front hallway.

"What happened to your footballer?" I yelled.

Dennis shrugged. "He took off somewhere with a girl." He paused. "It's sad. He has a wife in Bremen. Two kids."

We went into the hall, and when the door shut behind us, the music snapped off.

Suzy looked at us, still wide-eyed. She clutched her little blue bag as if it were about to be snatched away.

"That was awful", she said. "All those drugs. And the girls with no shirts on. And the men were saying such disgusting things!"

"Welcome to Germany", said Dennis.

Suzy glanced at him briefly, but it was to me that she turned. "I thought they were so cool", she muttered.

"This is what cool looks like up close", I said. "Come on, we have friends waiting in the King Kamehameha. Don't go home until you're cheered up."

"It isn't at all how I thought it would be", she said.

*   *   *

We took a cab to the King Kamehameha. Suzy asked Dennis about his studies. Dennis answered carefully, still in his Oxbridge pronunciation. It amused me; I listened to the sound rather than the words. One of his courses dealt with ethics, and the two exchanged platitudes.

Suzy tried him on Palestine, but Dennis dodged the topic with a dazzling smile. His grandfather was acquitted at Nuremburg.

There was a large crowd outside the club, and there were growls when we walked straight to the front, and Eberhardt let us through. Suzy, who had paid half the cab fare, offered to pay for us all. She had a surprisingly thick roll of banknotes in her little blue bag. We compromised by splitting Dennis' cover charge.

"I get to dance with him half the time", said Suzy, seizing his arm.

Dennis smiled smugly. "I am not for sale, by the way."

"It's a deal", I said. I was thinking mostly of my third gin and tonic.

Suzy bore Dennis away to the dance floor, and I slipped into the patio to look for Marcus and the others. Marcus was sitting at a table, its chairs claimed by jackets. I slid in beside him. He had been roped into watching the table while Kurt and Michael danced. I sent him away to the dance floor and waved the waitress over. While I waited for her to return with my drink, I looked around the twig-roofed room. My eye fell upon two women in hijab. They were sitting with young Turkish men in club clothes, and one of the women was Dennis' sister. Catching sight of me, she rose and came to my table.

"Is this place free?"

"Yes, certainly", I said.

Hannah, or Aisha, as she preferred, sat with her back facing her friends' table. "Can I have a cigarette?"

Marcus' pack was sitting on the table. I pushed it over. Aisha took out a cigarette and lit it with a tea light. She put the candle down again and took a drag. She looked at me through Dennis' eyes, and once again I was disconcerted to see them in that round, pale face, thinly fringed by strange blonde lashes. Was it ironic or obvious that the sibling who looked least Turkish would reclaim their (marginal) Turkish heritage? Were it not for the hijab, Aisha would be unmistakable for anyone but a German girl, blonde and stern. She used to smoke half a pack a day.

"He'll smell it on you", I said. I nodded in her husband's direction.

"It's smoky in here anyway", said Aisha. "I haven't seen you for a long time."

"I've been travelling a lot."

"I saw Dennis on the dance floor with a girl in a blue wig. Who's she?"

"A Canadian girl we met. She's nice."

"She looks young."

My age was a sore point with Aisha. She was used to calling the shots in her younger brother's life. When she was a traditionalist Catholic, her idea was that he should become a priest. Now that she was a Muslim, her idea was that he should become a Turk. My appearance had interfered with both those plans.

"She is young", I said. "Young and noisy."

"Don't you worry?" asked Aisha.

The waitress brought my drink, and I gave her some euros.

"I only worry about the old ones", I lied.

"Oh", said his sister with a snort. "Dennis always loved money."

"Very true."

"And that doesn't bother you?"

"Why should it? Millions do."

"I've often wondered how a journalist could afford to live the way you do."

"No harm in wondering."

Aisha pondered that and decided to go straight for the jugular. "How long are you going to be content with being my brother's whore?"

"Whore yourself. I'm paying the bills."

"My parents think you're going to marry him."

"No harm in thinking, either."

"You're divorced. Why not just do it?"

"According to your great-uncle, I'm still married. So why not ask him?"

"Uncle Franz doesn't know you're living together."

"Thank God for small mercies", I said in English.

"My mother says you're waiting for a Church divorce."

"It's not a divorce; it's an annulment."

"Why bother waiting for it if you're sleeping together anyway?"

"Anyone would think you wanted me to marry Dennis", I said. "I'm flattered."

"Don't be", said Aisha. "I'm just curious about your Catholic hypocrisy. You're on the Pill, too, aren't you?"

"*Das geht dich einen absoluten Scheissdreck an.*"

"He's my brother", she said stubbornly.

Over her head, I saw Dennis come into the room, Suzy still clinging to his arm. They were arguing amiably. Suzy evidently still wanted him to dance.

"Ask your brother then", I said. Jabbing out her cigarette, Aisha turned around.

Dennis stopped still in his tracks, and his face lit up with a surprised delight, dulled a second later by memory and trepidation. "Hannah!"

"Hallo, small one. Who's your new friend?"

"This is Suzy. She doesn't speak German. What are you doing here?"

"Tarkan wanted to come here with his buddies. I said if he goes, I go."

Suzy watched the exchange, smiling but not understanding a word. Aisha held her hand out and introduced herself in English. Suzy's smile widened, and she wrung Aisha's grasp.

"Wow!" she cried. "Nice to *meet* you!"

"Do you come from Toronto?" asked Aisha.

"Wow! How did you guess?"

"Dennis says that you are a student."

"Yes, I go to U of T. I mean the University of Toronto. I'm here on an exchange."

"And you are a peace activist", said Aisha. "Did you know that *Islam* means 'peace'?"

"I *did*", said Suzy. She sat herself down beside me and looked avidly at blue-eyed Aisha in her hijab.

Dennis excused himself and wandered over to the table of young Turkish men. He leaned toward his brother-in-law, and they shook hands. Tuning out Aisha and Suzy, I watched Dennis charm his sister's friends. Charm always came easily to Dennis.

We met in Kleinburg after his great-uncle's installation as the Archbishop. There was the high and solemn Mass in the ancient cathedral (rebuilt 1946), complete with processions of Scouts with banners and flags, ladies in black dresses and blue scarves, children in First Communion suits and white dresses, the Ladies of Malta in their black lace mantillas, the Knights of Malta with their hats tucked under their arms, a virtual army of altar boys, and a squadron of priests. A late supper at one of Kleinburg's ancient inns followed.

I was invited to supper as a representative of the rich American Catholic media outlet. The new Archbishop was surprised, not to say disconcerted, to learn that I was not American but a Scot. Later I discovered that his father had been imprisoned in a POW camp in Fife.

38

My German was still rough in spots, and I found the supper exceedingly tedious. The nun on my left was obsessed with women's ordination, and the priest on my right was full of gloomy predictions about the Church in Germany. It occurred to me more than once that I had been placed there to separate them. I had enough for my article, and I was wondering how soon I could politely leave, when I noticed, at the head table, a dark-haired young man staring at me. When he saw that he'd caught my eye, he smiled, and I felt rather dazzled. Embarrassed, I went back to my schnitzel, but I glanced up again, and the dark-haired young man smiled at me once more. This routine went on into the pudding course, and I found myself blushing. It seemed all very ridiculous. I was not even the youngest woman in the room. Then, to my mingled surprise and—yes, I admit it—delight, the young man got up and crossed over to my table. Ignoring the nun and the priest, he leaned over me.

"Good evening", he said in English. "Are you the English journalist?"

"Scots", I said in German and added, stupidly, "But I work for Americans."

"Ah", he said. "*Schottisch*. If you would permit me, I would like to show you a building of historical interest right across the street."

"Right now?"

"Yes, right now. It is going to rain, you understand."

I didn't understand, but I saw that he had his leather coat over his arm, so I picked up my own coat, shouldered my bag, and followed him obediently out of the room. At the door, he asked for my coat, and shook it open. Feeling very embarrassed (and not a little elated), I slipped it on.

The young man nodded and opened the door to the dark, cobble-stoned road. "It is not exactly across the street", he said. "It is a little further down."

At that, I paused. For a moment, I wondered if the young man weren't a charming maniac, and I imagined a ghastly tabloid headline, the photo of my plastic-wrapped corpse modestly reserved for page three.

"My name is Dennis Erlichmann, by the way", said the young man in English. "The Archbishop is my great-uncle."

"Oh", I said. "Er. Brilliant. I'm Catriona McClelland."

By way of answer, Dennis offered me his arm, and I self-consciously walked beside him, careful in high heels of the cobblestones. I decided that a woman was reasonably safe with an archbishop's great-nephew, at least in Kleinburg.

"Not much farther", said Dennis, and we walked another block into the heart of the town. There was a dance club nearby; I could hear trance music.

"Look here", I said in German. "Where exactly are we going anyway?"

"Almost there", replied Dennis. "You speak German very well. Which is your journalism school?"

"School?"

"And here we are", said Dennis, stopping outside the club. The bouncer outside looked us over and gave us a snaggle-toothed grin. "It looks historical, doesn't it?"

"Not particularly", I said. "It looks like a converted house built in the late forties."

"That's historical", said Dennis. "And I am inviting you."

"Inviting me where? Into the club? What about your great-uncle's dinner?"

"They'll never miss us. Besides, you were bored. Come on."

The bouncer pushed open the door. "*Heut' ist Mein Tag*" came blaring out and gathered us up. Dennis took my hand and led the way into the strobe-lit darkness.

"This is mental", I said. "All right, one hour."

Two years later, Dennis shook hands again with his brother-in-law and came back to my table. Aisha was now discoursing on the beauties of the Turkish language.

"Dennis could learn it, if only he weren't so lazy. He's very good at languages."

"Thank you", said Dennis. "But I am not lazy, by the way. I am busy."

"Dennis is an excellent student", said Aisha to Suzy. "My parents have great hopes for him."

Then she looked at me balefully. "He goes to too many parties."

"Parties? Me too. But man, I couldn't believe the party we just went to", exclaimed Suzy. "I almost died."

I tried to kick Suzy under the table but missed. As she described the party, piling on the details, Aisha's bland face got stonier and stonier, and she flashed daggerlike glances at me from under her sparse blonde lashes. This was not lost on Dennis, whose face became equally rigid. At last, he couldn't take it anymore. He swallowed the rest of my gin and tonic, made a face, and took my hand.

"Come", he said to me. "Let's dance."

We escaped to the dance floor. Marcus, Kurt, and Michael were nowhere to be seen, but we didn't care. The air vibrated with music; the beat ticked hypnotically. We carved out a space for ourselves on the dance floor where we could be alone, anonymous and safe from anything beyond sensory experience. The third G & T had done the trick; I was stoned. Nothing mattered except the beat, the music, and the man a handsbreadth away from me, smelling of sweat and musky cologne. Not even the anticipation of going home, once again, miraculously, with Dennis fluttered my euphoric trance. Two lines of John Donne's drifted into my emptied mind, rearranging themselves to suit my circumstances. Dennis was all states, and all rulers I. Nothing else was.

"Hey!" yelled Suzy, appearing at my side. "I guess we should go, eh? Aisha says Dennis has class in the morning."

Chapter 4

I looked out the bell-tower window to the darkening street below. Beside me, the young curate listened gloomily to his mobile, saying "klar" and "nein" at intervals. He was Polish and still spoke German with a strong Polish accent. He clung to the balustrade as if he were a kitten treed by a pack of wild dogs. From below came the sound of chanting, shouts, whistles, breaking bottles, and the sirens of police cars. I trained my binoculars down the street. Riot police, olive green and helmeted, were running to the scene from two directions. Here and there a trash bin burned merrily.

I looked for my photographer, Santosh. He had taken all the aerial shots he wanted and thought he'd try his luck on the edges of the riot.

The priest uttered a last dismal "*klar*" and hung up. He sighed heavily.

"How long has this been going on?"

"This is the third night in a row."

"Any Turks?"

"What?"

"Any Muslim demonstrators, or are they all Antifa?"

"Muslims demonstrating in Kreuzberg? You must be joking. This isn't Paris, thank God. There might be some Turks down there. I haven't gone to look."

"Have any of the activists requested to speak with you?"

"With me?" Pater Wolski's brown eyes widened. "Why would they want to speak to me?"

"Well, they are demonstrating outside your church."

"But I am only the curate", he said. "They might have called the pastor. I don't know." The pastor was on holiday in Prague, leaving the mostly Polish parish in Wolski's care. "I hope they don't get into the garage", he said. "The car is new."

"Send the bill to the Holy Father", I suggested.

"The Holy Father cannot be blamed", said Pater Wolski. "He didn't say anything that wasn't true."

"'Without a recollection of her Christian faith, Germany will disintegrate into a dark sea of hedonism, apathy, and perhaps ultimately bloodshed.' You wouldn't call those types down there apathetic, would you, Pater?"

"Half my family was killed by German fascists", said the priest morosely. "I never imagined I'd be surrounded by German anti-fascists."

There was an explosion. Pater Wolski flinched. I looked to the right.

"Just a smoke bomb."

"*Dobry Boze!*"

I caught sight of a Palestinian scarf, but the wearer was a beefy blond. He whipped a rock at a police van. The police formed two cordons along the right and left sides of the church square. The rioters bellowed and threw rocks and bottles.

"Come on, Turks", I said impatiently in English. "Get tore in."

"Why are you so interested in Turks?" said the priest pettishly. I forgot he knew some English. "They're communists, I tell you, not jihadists."

"My editor isn't interested in communists. He's interested in Muslims. And not the seculars. The religious kind. The kind we have interreligious dialogues with. Or who blow up trains. Either way."

"They don't protest here", said Pater Wolski. "Maybe Hamburg?"

"There's Santosh", I said. He was stationed behind a row of green-and-brown recycling cans to the right side of the square. His was the only brown face to be seen.

The cordon of police began to run forward, and the youth began to scatter through the park before the church. Others held their ground. The shouting and whistling intensified. Bottles clattered against the helmets and smashed on the ground. The police began to whack the protestors with truncheons while other protestors tried to stop them. Santosh popped up and, after taking shots of the beatings, ran with the refugees through the park. He was a very good photographer and, as it happened, a very good Catholic. This was his parish church. His phone call got me into the bell tower in the first place.

I had come into Berlin by train and gone straight to Kreuzberg, checking into the hotel where Dennis and I had once stayed. That was a mistake: the moment I stepped into the lobby I felt a wave of homesickness. I fought the impulse to send him a text message and hurried to the

43

church, deftly avoiding dog droppings and litter and just managing not to be run over by cyclists. Cars pumped hip-hop, German and American, into the street, and young men everywhere wore baggy pants and baseball caps askew. Kreuzberg was its usually ratty self, its anarchist spirit barely touched by the new bistros and classy bars.

The church was a bit of a mess. Several windows had been smashed; others had fist-sized holes in them. The wooden front doors were slightly singed, and the stone porch looked as though someone had built a bonfire there. Anti-Nazi and anti-papal graffiti besmirched the outer walls. But for whatever reason, the adjoining rectory had been spared. I rang the doorbell, and Santosh opened the door.

"Come in", he said in his heavy accent. "I've been cheering up the Father."

The Father was a short, thin, prematurely balding man in his late twenties. He had dark shadows under his eyes, not having slept a wink, he said, in two and a half days. He couldn't get the pastor on the phone, and his bishop had told him to stay put. He was terrified that his younger parishioners were going to organise a counterprotest. Meanwhile, he didn't trust the police to adequately guard the church while he carried out his duties. He suspected them of being communists. Berlin was full of communists; he had been shocked when he first came to Germany. He had been worried about neo-Nazis, not communists. But every May 1 began a new season of Antifa agitprop and protests. He was not happy when I suggested that we keep watch in the bell tower in case the protestors came back again. However, he had heard of both my media group and me and eventually consented.

Two riot cops wrestled the beefy blond to the ground. A third hovered over him with a truncheon. The youth shouted and spat on their boots. They dragged him away to one of the white-and-green vans.

"They are spoiled kids", said Pater Wolski. "They are spitting on freedom, I think. So stupid. They lack for nothing except God. They are looking for God, but they do not even know it. May I borrow your binoculars?"

"Of course", I said. From where I stood, I could see the remains of the Berlin Wall with the unaided eye. I made some notes. My editor couldn't care less about communists, but spoiled European youths who lacked for nothing except God might go over well.

"Any sign of your youth group?"

"No, thank God", said the priest. He shuddered. "It is terrible, terrible. Why do the police not use water cannons? Dobry Boze! That was a girl."

Angry female screams drifted upward. Another smoke bomb exploded.

"What percentage of your parish would you say is under forty years of age?"

"I am not sure. Half?"

"That's a lot for Germany."

"They are mostly foreigners, like me."

"Poles?"

"Poles, Indians, Czechs, Slovaks, Vietnamese."

"Filipinos?"

"Yes, of course."

"How many young Germans?"

"Is this important?"

"It's evidently important to the Holy Father."

The priest furled his balding brow. "There are some. But this is an immigrant neighbourhood, you understand. And most of the young Germans here are communists and anarchists. They are students. Leftists."

"What do you believe is at the heart of the alienation of German youth from the Church?"

Pater Wolski lowered my binoculars and stared at me with his big, round, frightened kitten eyes. "Are you serious?"

"Not really, but I have to write something."

"Communism", said the priest. "Berlin is still in East Germany, after all. The Wall fell, but what has replaced it? Their parents didn't know Christ; their grandparents didn't know Christ; how can they know Christ?"

"Yes, but the churches in West Germany aren't exactly packed either."

"It is as the Holy Father said. Hedonism, materialism—"

"Hypocrisy?"

Pater Wolski looked alarmed, as if I had morphed into a communist. "What do you mean?"

"Well, so many German Catholics are divorced and remarried, use artificial birth control, live together before marriage ..."

"Ah", interrupted the priest. "That is the same all over western Europe. It is very sad. It is even so in Britain, is it not?"

"Sort of", I said. "But at least we worry about it. The younger generation of Catholics—the ones who go to Church, I mean—is more traditional. They like rules."

"That is good", said the priest. "The young need structures. Otherwise, they are confused and aimless. Their lives lack meaning. The drugs, the sex, the music—it is all an escape from meaninglessness."

"An escape, certainly."

The youths were mostly dispersed. The yelling and smashing faded into the distance. They would either go home or regroup somewhere else. I decided to go outside and wait for Santosh. The priest followed me down the narrow stairs to the church and led the way back to the priests' living quarters. Pater Wolski shook my hand limply before I slipped out the rectory door. He shut it, and I heard the slam of a bolt and the rattle of a chain.

A riot cop was stationed by the rectory stairs, around the building from the scene of action. He looked at me briefly and nodded. I nodded back. The sky was clear. It would be a fine night, I said to the cop, and he agreed. I offered him a cigarette (packed for such an eventuality), and he accepted. He took his helmet off. I took a cigarette myself, to be companionable.

"Who are you?" he asked.

"I'm writing about the riots", I said.

"Are you a *Wessi*?"

"No, Scots."

He said I spoke German very well. I thanked him, and we smoked on. I was wondering how to broach the topic when he brought it up himself. "It's not like the anti-fascists to demonstrate three nights in a row."

"Not like in France", I said.

"That's not Antifa; that's Muslims."

"And Muslims don't demonstrate here?"

"Not yet."

"Is it coming?"

"Don't quote me."

"Milli Görüs? Or someone new?"

"*Tja*", said the cop. "Who's this? A pal of yours?"

Santosh was limping up the street. He waved. The cop threw his cigarette on the ground and put his helmet back on.

"No photographs", he said.

The rioters had gone to Orienplatz, Santosh reported. A bottle had smashed against his knee. Nevertheless, he was cheerful. He had taken some very good photographs. I bid good night to the cop and went with Santosh to his car, parked safely in a distant garage near the Spree.

"Did you get any names?" I asked.

Santosh tapped his pocket. "Right here. I got tickets to the after-party, too."

"Santosh, I love you. Leave Birgitte and marry me."

"She'd kill both of us. Forget it."

I read the graffiti-covered walls as we passed them. A lot of the writing was in English. In some ways, Kreuzberg wanted desperately to be American, for all that it railed against American imperialism.

"Why three nights, Santosh? Three nights at the same place?"

"No idea", said Santosh.

"Is it trinitarian?"

Santosh laughed. "I doubt they would know what that means."

We drove across the river into East Berlin and plunged into the long purgatory of concrete blocks. The after-party was in one of the last squats, a three-sided building with a courtyard. A defaced brick wall divided it from the street. The building itself was covered in luminous drawings, mottoes, and banners. Along one side of the building, some philosopher had written, "The border that divides is not between people but between the top and the bottom."

"Transcendence over immanence", I said.

"What's that?"

"Theology. It's very Lutheran, what they have there."

Santosh snorted and parked the car. He left most of his equipment in the boot. Our hosts knew we were journalists, so Santosh brought a camera. The squatters greeted Santosh with enthusiasm but me with reserve until I deliberately began to play up my accent and make grammatical mistakes. They liked that.

There was a distinctly carnival air. There were grills set up on either side of the courtyard, and the smell of sausage filled the air. Vegetarianism is not a dogma of German anarchism. Pale bodies in army fatigues and thrift-shop garments flitted before me. A stereo system set into a lower window poured alternative metal into the air. The air was now distinctly chilly, and I wished I had worn a thicker jacket.

47

I looked for a person with some badge of authority and found a girl with a donation box. She had fuzzy blonde dreadlocks tied with red ribbons.

"Magic?" asked Santosh.

"He's inside. Flat 91C", said the girl.

The hallways were heavy with incense and marijuana. I thought fleetingly of Dennis. He would like to visit this squat, maybe stay a week to say he had, but in the end, he would return to the peace and order of our flat in Bornheim.

There was no door on Flat 91C. The room was lit with red bulbs, and everywhere the young and not-so-young sat on cushions or beaten-up furniture, talking and drinking beer. Santosh knew a surprising number of these people and introduced me as a British journalist, not mentioning my name. And at last we came to the anarchist hero, sitting on a battered, brown leather chair that had stuffing coming out. He was frowning as he listened to two boys argue loudly, and he picked at the stuffing. Magic was in his late twenties, was the editor of the indie paper *Neu!* and carried on a public war with his father, who held some minor portfolio in the Reichstag. He was a nondescript youth, brown-haired and sallow. He had an improvised bandage around his hand, made of a ripped white T-shirt, and I wondered if he had been hurt at the demonstration.

When he saw Santosh, the hero scowled. "No photos!"

Santosh looked surprised, but his smile dimmed only a watt or two. "Hi, Magic. Great protest. This is my buddy. She's a journalist from London."

"Edinburgh", I said.

"No interviews."

"But she's come all the way from Frankfurt."

"I don't care. Get her out of here."

He stood up, and his friends did the same. The smile slid from Santosh's face. He looked so astonished, it would have been comical in other circumstances. Magic was one of the all-time publicity whores. I, however, was remembering Antifa's commitment to violence as a means to combat fascists, capitalists, and just about everyone not a member of Antifa.

"Hey, that's cool", I said in my worst Scots-German. "No problem. I have only one question, anyway. Why picket the same church three days running?"

Fear flickered in Magic's eyes before they hardened. "I said get out", he said in English.

"All right then", I said, idiotically. "Cheerio."

I turned right around and made as graceful an exit as I could, given that we were being hurried along by Magic's growling friends. Beside me, Santosh protested good-naturedly.

"No elevator", said Magic when we reached the hall. "Down the stairs."

My heart jumped at that. Gruesome possibilities occurred to me at once. I looked sideways at Santosh, but he was still amiably reminding Magic and his boys of all his street credibility.

Magic pushed me through the stairwell door, and his buddies shoved Santosh. I caught the railing, and Santosh fell into me.

"Now run", shouted the anarchist hero. "Run!"

His voice echoed through the narrow stairwell, and we ran, Magic's boys hooting and cursing from above. We didn't stop running until we had burst into the courtyard, where we slowed to a swift stroll. Someone tried to give me a beer; I shook my head, breathless. I looked up at the red-lit window of 91C. Magic was staring down at us, watching our retreat.

"How very strange", said Santosh.

"I can think of better words. Keep walking."

The car was untouched, I was relieved to see. We got in wordlessly, and Santosh drove back to West Berlin. He was embarrassed by his failure. Santosh prided himself on knowing everyone in Berlin under thirty who made news. I could see that his feelings were hurt, too. He was a likeable guy, and he loved to be liked.

"Where do we go next?"

"My hotel", I said. "I'm going to file my story, and then I'm going to bed."

"There's something weird going on", said Santosh.

"Whatever it is, it will have to go on without me. Anarchists, communists, my editor doesn't care. Find me a nice Muslim riot next time."

"There aren't any in Berlin."

"Well, an anti-Semitic imam then. If you can find one who preaches in German."

"They don't."

"Any pals in al-Qaeda?"

"You must be joking."

"Al-Qaeda might be too much for my editor, too, come to think of it."

Santosh let me off in front of the hotel, and I wearily walked in. The familiar smell once again reminded me of Dennis. Expense be hanged, I would call him as soon as I got to my room. I made a mental bet with myself that he was at a club.

A figure curled up in a chair by the concierge's desk uncurled. I looked twice. It was Suzy, wigless. Her dark hair, streaked with scarlet, was pulled into a short ponytail. A red rucksack, Canadian flag firmly sewed on, was at her feet.

"Catriona!" she said. "I thought you would never come."

* * *

She looked so tired and relieved, I forgot about the monstrous bank-roll in her bag the other night. At that moment, she seemed like a child, one of the girls I had occasionally minded as a teenager.

"How on earth did you get here?" I asked.

"I hitchhiked", she said. "People here sure speak a lot of English."

"Hitchhiked! From Frankfurt? What on earth possessed you?"

"I wanted to get to Berlin."

"You're crazy."

"The people were really nice", said Suzy. "First there was a businessman going to Dresden, and then there were some students going to Leipzig, and then there was a trucker going to Berlin."

"God in heaven. You got into cars alone with men? How could you?"

"I was careful", she said.

"Why on earth didn't you take a train or the bus?"

"I'm trying to save money", said Suzy, shyly. She looked at the night porter, who was reading a sports paper. I remembered the bank-roll and wondered how long it was meant to last her.

"I guess you'll want to stay with me then", I said.

"Yes", she said. "I would be totally grateful."

"Well, come along."

Suzy leapt up, profuse in her thanks, and shouldered her rucksack. The night porter was a tolerant chap. I offered to sign Suzy in, but he sent us on our way with a wink. As I discovered later, Suzy had told him that she was my niece.

The room had a double bed and a pullout couch. Suzy dropped her rucksack by the couch and disappeared into the WC. I took my laptop from its bag in the closet, placed it on the desk, and began to write my story. Suzy came galumphing into the room. She asked if I minded if she took a shower. I said I wouldn't mind anything she did so long as she remained absolutely silent until I filed my article. Chastened, Suzy disappeared back into the WC. After that, I forgot her. When I write, I am deaf to everything except voices demanding my attention. Dennis had learned long ago not to bother me, and I had become accustomed to blocking out the bleep-bleep of his video games. Thus, I was momentarily surprised when, after sending the story to my editor in New York, I turned to see Suzy sitting on the couch. She looked at me with big eyes.

"Finished?" she asked.

"Finished", I said. "I didn't mean to keep you up. You should have gone to bed."

"I didn't feel like sleeping."

She seemed nervous, and I wondered why.

"Remind me again", I said. "Why did you come to Berlin?"

"Well, there were two reasons", she said.

"What's the first reason?"

"Well, I heard you and Silke talking about the anti-Pope riots, and it sounded interesting."

"Why? Are you Catholic?"

"Well, I was born Catholic", said Suzy cautiously. "I'm not anymore. It was kind of pointless, you know?"

"I don't know", I said. "Being Catholic is many things, but I've never found it pointless."

"Well, that's it", said Suzy. "Like, what is Catholicism anyway? I mean, look at my parents. We went to church sometimes and all that, but it drove me crazy. All those people standing around saying things that they don't believe. And going up for Communion like they're in line at a buffet. If I thought that *really* was God up there, I wouldn't be able to go up. I'd be terrified. And all those rules that no one obeys anyway. It's so stupid. My parents say they're Catholic, but they break the rules like everybody else. My dad got remarried at City Hall."

"Look not on our sins, but on the faith of Your Church."

"What?"

"Maybe they try not to break the rules."

51

Suzy made a face. "Whatever. I want a religion I can really believe in, you know? Like I don't believe Jesus was God. I think he was just a very good man, like Muhammad, you know?"

"I'm a Catholic myself", I said, all too aware that I was proving Suzy's point about Catholics. Perhaps she sensed my embarrassment because she hurriedly added that a lot of Catholics were really good people and meant well, even some priests.

"Well", I said, trying for a lighthearted tone. "What was your second reason for coming to Berlin?"

Suzy blushed and stared at the orange carpet. "Well, I came to see you."

"To see me?"

"Yes."

"Why?"

"I'm afraid to tell you", she said. "Promise me you won't get too mad. I know you'll be a little mad, but please don't be too mad."

"About what?"

She looked up from the carpet, her eyes brimming. "This is totally embarrassing, but I'm in love with Dennis."

To my credit, I didn't laugh. I just stared at her. She sniffled and brushed at her eyes with the back of her hand. For lack of anything to say, I went over to the bedside table and picked up the tissue box. I handed it to her.

"Thank you", said Suzy.

I sat down at the desk again. At last I said, to make sure I had the facts, "My Dennis?"

Suzy nodded miserably.

I bit my bottom lip to stop myself from smiling. It was so absurd. "Couldn't you have waited to tell me until I got back to Frankfurt?"

"I didn't know when you were coming back."

"How did you even know I was here?"

"I called Dennis", said Suzy. "He gave me his number that night, and this morning I called him. I don't have your number."

"Well, he could have told you when I'm coming back. Suzy, does he know you came rushing out here?"

"No", said Suzy emphatically. "I didn't tell him anything. I just asked if I could talk to you, and he said you were in Berlin, and I asked where, and he told me. And I got nervous and hung up."

"So you didn't tell him of your feelings?"

"Of course not", said Suzy. "How could I, without telling you first?"

"That's how it's generally done", I said. "Although most women wouldn't blurt it right out. When did this first happen?"

"It was at the King Kamehameha. When we were dancing. I mean, he just looked down at me and smiled, and I thought I would faint, you know? And afterwards, on my way home, I mean, I felt so bad because he's your boyfriend."

"I see."

"And I think it was seeing all those cute guys at that guy Gustav's place. I mean, they were cute, but kind of slimy too, and I wondered, what if Dennis ends up like that? Gustav, Florian, the guy who was hitting on me—they were kind of gross. And I thought, Dennis needs to get away from all that. This will sound weird, but I thought he needed protecting."

"Have you been talking to Aisha?"

"Yes, she called me the next day. She's really nice. I went to her place, and it was so cool, you know? I mean she's religious, seriously religious, but she's also fun. Anyway, she's really worried about Dennis. And I felt terrible, listening to her talk about him, because of being in love with him and not being able to say anything. And I never would have said anything, even to you, if you guys were married. I mean, I'm not like that. I believe in marriage, you know? It sucks that my parents divorced."

"There are commitments other than marriage", I said. For the first time, she had annoyed me. "Some are quite serious."

"Cat", said Suzy. "Dennis said you were getting married, and you said you weren't. How come?"

"Because we aren't", I said. "Dennis is twenty-two. That's a little young for getting married, don't you think? Even in Canada it's rare."

"The Muslim kids do."

"Dennis isn't a Muslim", I said. "And whatever Aisha says, he's a typical German. The only thing that makes him any different from the others is that he sometimes goes to church."

"I'm twenty-two," said Suzy, "and if Dennis asked me to marry him, I'd be the happiest woman in the world."

"You don't even know him", I said, but the words sounded foolish even in my ears. That didn't matter to Suzy. That hadn't mattered to me either, two years ago, when Dennis talked his way into my flat one night and refused to leave.

"I'm going to ask him to choose between us", said Suzy. "It's the only way I can live with myself. I want to be one hundred percent honest. You know, I've told so many lies in my life. Sometimes they're kind of necessary. But I never want to lie, or even pretend, to you or Dennis. Do you know what I mean, Cat?"

"Oh, Suzy. Is that necessary? Dennis and I have been lovers for two years. That gives me quite an advantage, you know."

Suzy looked up at me, still dabbling at her eyes with the wad of tissues, and I suddenly saw myself as I must have appeared to her. My hair was a slightly different shade at the roots; I have been dying it since I was twenty-six. There was the crease between my eyebrows, the gouge beside my mouth. Faint rings had gradually appeared on my neck; I saw Suzy considering them. In her reality, older women lost younger men to younger women, not vice versa. And for the first time in her presence, I felt the chill of fear of loss. It was ridiculous, of course, but all the same . . . Was this not why I had kept Dennis at arm's length as long as I could hold out against him?

"Nein, Deniz, ich bin zu alt für dich. Mensch, ich bin zweiunddreissig."

"Das ist mir scheissegal."

"Deniz, Du gehst jetzt nach Hause."

"Ich bin zu hier."[1]

Suzy blew her nose.

"Well, I'm just not going to lie", she said. "And I feel a lot better now. Thanks for not freaking out, Cat. I think I can sleep now. I kept waking up all night last night thinking about what I was going to say to you."

"Well, you've said it, so stop worrying. These things happen to everybody." And at last I gave into ill-will, revenge for the line at my mouth and the rings around my neck. I said, "Women fall in love with Dennis all the time. We're used to it."

"Oh", said Suzy. "I guessed that. I could tell from the way he moves his head."

I felt like I'd been slapped. I stared at her. "Whatever do you mean?"

"He's got a massive vain streak", said the girl. "It's kind of girly. But I don't care. It's not his face I'm in love with. Well," she smiled, as if conceding a point, "not just his face. It's his soul I'm after."

---

[1] "Deniz, no. I am too old for you. I'm thirty-two."
"I don't care."
"Deniz, go home."
"I am home."

"You can't have his soul", I said. "It's fine where it is."

"Oh God", said Suzy. "I'm sorry, Cat. I forgot. Of course, you love him too."

"Quite."

Suzy laughed now, released from nervousness.

"*Quite*", she repeated. "That's what I love about you, Cat. You're so controlled, so restrained. It's like you never lose your cool at all."

"How very reassuring for everybody."

"I think it's great. Do you think the bed pulls out this way?"

By the time I turned off the lamps, Suzy was already asleep. Her young face glowed on the pillow like mother-of-pearl. Mine must have done the same once; no one ever told me. I lay awake for a very long time, staring into the darkness.

Chapter 5

I planned to leave Berlin the next day, but a sandwich shop in Lehrter Bahnhof blew up at 5:00 AM, killing its Turkish German owner. The world turned its attention to Kreuzberg, and no journalist worth her salt could leave it. But Suzy left town that morning; she had fulfilled her mission—to announce her love for Dennis—and there was nothing to keep her. I left her asleep when the call came in at 5:30, and when I returned from the press scrum around the train station, she was gone. I assumed that she had gone to see the sights, chat up fellow peaceniks, and browse the shops of Kreuzberg. She was as incapable of seeing how bombed shops might affect her as she was incapable of understanding how her own political activities might hurt others. Weeks later, I went berserk and rubbed her face in it, and I remember how she touched her face and said, "I guess I should wash up." I knew then that she was tidily arranging her thoughts according to the lectures she had been taught: that the West was bad, that the West had brought terror upon itself. Yet she never meant anyone any harm, and in the end she died for her beliefs in the Main River.

It was only when I returned to Frankfurt that I learned how Suzy, while I elbowed my way into the acrid underground station, had hitched a ride back. This time she was lucky and found someone going directly to Sachsenhausen. She must have stopped at an Internet café on the way, for I discovered that she had sent me an email which I read when I returned, tired, to my Kreuzberg hotel.

"Omg, Cat", she wrote. "U r so cool. Thks so much 4 lst nite. I was freaken! You could have kicked my ass but u didn't. Now I feel ok in myself. Don't worry. I'm not going to talk to Dennis til u get back. Whtever hppns, I want us 2 B friends K! C U in Frkfrt. Suzy."

It wasn't the dodgy spelling that annoyed me as much as the idea that Suzy thought she could just waltz off with my boyfriend. Is her generation more confident than mine? When I was Suzy's age, I was afraid to talk to any stranger, let alone foreigners. It was a shock to discover that men found my lean frame and green eyes attractive. It was another shock to discover that someone as handsome as Dennis could be in love with me, even after he found out how old I was. Dennis had always been confident of his love for me, but I, older and wiser, had been rather less so. All I could do was try to postpone the inevitable, to scare off the cougars and intimidate my younger rivals. I hadn't doubted that one day Dennis would leave me for a younger woman. But I never foresaw that I would hold Dennis as he cried over the death of Suzy Davis.

I went out that night—I had nothing better to do—to visit Santosh's youth group. The church was off limits; there were still policemen guarding it. So instead, the youth met in one of Kreuzberg's old cheap beer halls and ordered towers of pale amber liquid. There was an American student with them, a blond German American from Cincinnati, Ohio. He spoke German well, although his vocabulary was out of date and he had a strong American accent. The Polish Germans joked him about it mercilessly although their own German was hardly of the purest. They were all talking excitedly about the Antifa protests and the "Bahnhof Bombing", as the papers called it, but I found it hard to follow the conversation: I kept thinking of Dennis and the thought: What if Suzy is right, and Dennis leaves me for her—what will I do?

One of the ethnic Germans said, "For sure, there will be pressure on the government to bring the troops home from Afghanistan. It is ridiculous for us to continue helping the Americans fight their imperialist war."

He ignored the American—Jason, I thought his name was—although the Polish Germans looked at him sidelong.

"But Afghanistan is not an imperialist war", said a Polish German girl. "The government of Afghanistan asked us to come. And it is not just Germany and the Americans who are there. The British are there, the Danes, even the Canadians."

"*Ach*, the British", said the German, Marko, with a shrug. "They do whatever the Americans tell them to do."

"Not exactly", I said. "And the Canadians certainly don't. They fight on their own schedule."

"Catriona is a Canadian", said Santosh, quite unnecessarily. Perhaps he thought it best that I not be British in that particular group. Jason looked in my direction and decided to take his resentment out on me.

"So when did a Canadian last die for his country?" he sneered.

"Last week", I said coolly. "In Kandahār. If you can call dying for the Afghans dying for his country."

"That's exactly it", said Marko eagerly. "What was he doing there? What are we doing there? And what are the British and Americans doing in Iraq?"

That was the red-hot issue. I would have thought that a nice Catholic youth group would have left the subject of Iraq alone in front of an American guest, but American so-called imperialism is an obsession with European students.

"I tell you what it is", said another young man—Czech, I think. "It's a class war. Everybody knows that the top Americans are getting rich off the wars. The war is being fought by the American poor to make more money for the American rich."

"That's Iraq", said the Polish German girl. "Not Afghanistan. The Taliban are really bad guys, you know. They tore out women's fingernails if they wore nail polish."

"The Taliban did business with an American President's oil company", said the Czech. "It's about oil, too, you know. It's all about oil. Thousands of poor and working-class soldiers are dying in Iraq and Afghanistan for oil and kickbacks to the contractors."

"And countless more Iraqis and Afghans are being killed, too", said Marko, not to be outdone by the Czech. "All of this is a useless waste of life."

He thumped the table.

I could see that the American Jason was getting redder and redder. Frankly, I couldn't understand why he just sat there and listened to all this. After all, it wasn't Germans who were being killed in Iraq and in Afghanistan; they were up in the relatively safe north. The south was where the heavy fire was, and it was the Americans and Canadians who were dying there.

"It isn't just poor and working-class soldiers", said the Polish German girl. Her name was Tina, and she sat beside Jason. I wondered idly if she were Jason's girlfriend. "My friend's boyfriend is in Afghanistan. His parents are rich."

"An officer", said the Czech dismissively.

"So what?" said Tina. "He could be killed too. This isn't about class. It's about social justice. Okay, the Americans shouldn't be in Iraq—the Iraqis had nothing to do with 9/11—but the Taliban hid

Osama Bin Laden, and when the Americans bombed Afghanistan, everybody cheered. The women could show their faces. The children could fly kites. And if nobody fights for them, the Taliban will come back again."

"But it shouldn't be Germany", said Marko. "It used to be illegal. The only reason why we have an army at all is to protect our own borders. It was stupid to get involved in Bosnia; it left us open for more foreign operations. The young people are against our military presence in Afghanistan, and it is the young people who have to fight."

"And only the poor and uneducated go into the ranks", said the Czech. "Look at how few guys do their military service. Only the guys too lazy and dumb to write their pacifist essay to the draft board do it."

"My boyfriend did his military service", I said, suddenly angry. "He didn't think it was fair to get out of it when his father and uncles did theirs. He had an uncle fighting for the French in Vietnam. And two of his great-uncles died at Stalingrad, by the way. One was shot down in Spain during the Civil War. So a year in an army office didn't seem like such a big deal to him. There was no question of his being sent to Afghanistan."

Santosh choked on his beer, and the youth group sat in an embarrassed silence. Jason looked at me like there might be hope for a Canadian after all.

"Dennis?" said Santosh. "Dennis did his military service?"

I could see him struggling to imagine Dennis as a recruit, dressed in grey, deprived of hair products.

"When he was eighteen", I said and sighed. The fight had gone out of me just as quickly as it had gone in. I started thinking about Suzy again. "He liked basic training, but he said everything else was boring." The Catholic chaplain had made passes at him, too, but I didn't think it was fair to burden the kids with that.

"*Wirklich*", said Jason in his thick American accent. Virk-lish. "Your boyfriend's uncle was in the Condor Legion?"

"His great-uncle", I said.

"Those guys were tough", said Jason in English. I could see he was enjoying the squirms of the youth group, and I had had enough. I told them all that it was interesting to hear what young Catholics thought of foreign policy and got up. Jason got up, too, and followed me to the door of the beer hall. A flicker of jealous panic passed over Tina's face, and I felt sorry for her.

"Those guys don't know what the hell they're talking about", said Jason in English. "Europeans are like children. They live in a fantasy-land, know what I'm saying? This bombing today. You know what the papers are going to write? Get the hell out of Afghanistan. And that's why the terrorists did it. Look at Spain. The Muslims know the Europeans are soft."

"I don't think the Germans are so soft", I said. "And what makes you so sure this was an Islamist bomb today anyway?"

"Aw, come on", said Jason. "Who else?"

"Antifa, the Nazis . . ."

"Not the Nazis", he said confidently, and suddenly I thought I understood Jason, and something inside me shrank away from him. I kept my face neutral, but Jason might have suspected I had guessed, for he said, "And you're right. Not all the Germans are soft."

"My boyfriend's pretty tough anyway", I lied. I concocted three equally tough brothers for Dennis, all big, bad-tempered Hessians with underground connections, always in trouble with the law. Jason listened with respect and gave me his business card. Business cards were a big fad for German students that year. I thanked him and put it in my wallet without looking at it. He drifted to the others, and I made a mental note to have a word with Santosh the next day. I looked at the card when I was safely back in my hotel room. There was no name: just an Iron Cross and a phone number. I felt vaguely ill and wondered how soon I could leave Berlin.

I put the card back in my wallet and wondered if it was illegal even to possess such a thing. As an EU citizen, I couldn't be deported—at least, I hoped I couldn't be deported. Getting myself kicked out of Germany would mean a victory by default for Suzy; and there, when I flipped open my laptop and checked my email, was indeed my Glencoe—the news of my promotion to bureau chief in Vatican City.

I sat on my pristine hotel bed with my laptop balanced on the pillow. From down the hall came the sound of a door closing and water running. As my stomach heaved, I read the news again. I was to be the bureau chief in Vatican City, the first woman ever so to be, and winkle information out of the notoriously difficult Vatican Press office. The Dominican Sisters of the Holy Sepulchre had agreed to house me until I found a flat; I would have my own little guest bedroom and eat in the kitchen set aside for boarders. Some of the Sisters were Germans, and I wondered whether Dennis' great-uncle knew anything about this. I wondered, in fact, if I had been kicked upstairs. I was to be a female bureau chief, a pioneer, an "influential laywoman", and in return for this career triumph, I would lose Dennis. Suzy had her entire study year before her, and after that, glamorous North America, whereas, according to the email, I had only two months to wrap things up in Frankfurt. Almost no one in Germany cares if you live with your boyfriend; the rules are rather more stringently applied in Vatican City. And Dennis was two years away from graduation.

The night was still early for Berlin, and I walked out of the hotel with no very clear idea of where I wanted to go. I was sick of Kreuzberg; I knew that much. Stumbling across a taxi stand, I told the Turkish driver to take me to Unter den Linden. He was listening to whiny Turkish pop music, and I wondered what he thought of the Bahnhof bombing. Was he secular or religious? Had he known the sandwich vendor? Was he afraid of a neo-Nazi backlash? Thinking about the plight of the Turks in Germany distracted me from the plight of one particular expat Scot. I told the driver to drop me outside the Hotel Adlon (rebuilt 1997), and I went straight to the bar. There I saw Petra Schattschneider and a whole host of other journalists I knew from Frankfurt. The "Bahnhof Bombing" was going to be a big story, all right. Depending on what came out, it might be front page for a week. Petra turned around and waved me over.

"I'm inviting you", she said. "Gin and tonic?"

"Sounds good."

We both had a gin and tonic, and then we had another. All around us, the men were drinking beer, and the place was full of noise. It seemed impossible that my life was going to be completely different in two months, that instead of standing around in this German bar drinking gin and talking terrorism with Petra Schattschneider while German men joked and bellowed, I'd be living in an Italian convent, looking for a flat. I fought the sense that I'd be walled up alive like a heroine in a hysterically anti-Catholic thriller.

I said, "I have to leave Germany."

"Interesting assignment?" asked Petra.

"No. Just Rome."

PART TWO

Chapter 1

Suzy had invited herself over for coffee, and I was momentarily startled by this Canadian assault on my home. The week after the Bahnhof bombing had been a bewildering kaleidoscope of press conferences, rallies, riots, and booze-ups wherever newsmen gathered. Throughout eastern Germany, neo-Nazis had quiet demonstrations, broken up violently by anti-Nazis. Magic had been detained by police; his father was bombarded with questions in the Reichstag. Then a top German footballer was charged with possession of cocaine, the Bahnhof bombing was driven to page three, and I went home to Dennis and rest.

Suzy's bizarre declaration, as the weeks wore on, seemed more and more like a joke or even a cover-up for her presence in Berlin. Peace Now had some funny friends, as I had heard during the week. Some Palestinian organization or other. Something Saudi. Perhaps Suzy had really dropped by to protest against the Pope in solidarity with Antifa.

I kept quiet about my email from New York. Dennis and I had only two more months together, and I wanted to keep at least one of them free from the old argument. I didn't even tell anyone at the office that I had been promoted, for fear that Dennis would hear about it from someone else.

I told him, "Suzy's coming by this afternoon."

Dennis grimaced. "*Na und?* I'll stay late at school then."

"She'd probably like to see you", I said. "She likes you."

"She likes my *sister*", said Dennis. "She goes for dinner at her house all the time. She talks about Islam, politics, Palestine. All the usual boring stuff that my sister likes."

"Well, don't stay away just because she's here."

"If she wants to see me, she can come to the KK. She probably wants to talk to you about her group. They've been doing big things."

"What kind of big things?"

"Oh, you know. Protests, rallies, lectures. She tried to bring in a guy from the Palestinian Authority, but the government wouldn't let him in. Something to do with Black November."

"Black September", I said. "Speakers cost money. Where is it coming from?"

"I don't know", said Dennis. "But they say she has a lot. She travels a lot, too. Berlin. Hamburg. Köln."

"Does she hitchhike?"

"Kurt says she went to Hamburg with some guy in a flashy car."

"That's a long drive", I said.

When Dennis left for class, I wrote a long email to my boss in New York. Usually words come easily to me. This time I wrote and erased, wrote and erased. The clichés and hyperbole piled up: "at this point in time", "a new epoch", "a burgeoning crisis", "a struggle to the death for the Christian roots of Europe". Essentially, I wanted to persuade my boss that the company needed to keep me squarely in Frankfurt, a few hours away from any western European Catholic town, the better to keep tabs on what was left of the Church in western Europe. My German was superior to my Italian; our man in Vatican City was doing a superlative job. A truly international Catholic news service needed someone who knew Germany as well as I did. Germany and nearby France were where the Church in Europe would blossom—as it had once again in 1817—or perish. But of course what I was mostly thinking was of a whitewashed cell in the Dominican convent, and Dennis going to bed with Suzy.

Writing lies is difficult for me, and to get back into a groove, I typed out the erasable truth: "Leaving Frankfurt would be an emotional disaster for me. I have a twenty-two-year-old live-in lover, and he has at least two more years of school here. He is closely related to a leading German prelate, so taking him with me to Rome is out of the question. As it is, our relationship has effectively ended my career as a writer of pious Catholic books, and if this were not so, I would rather resign from the company than go to Rome. Meanwhile, my lover is an extraordinarily handsome young man, and without my influence, he might be drawn into the drug- and sex-crazed world of the international jet set."

For a minute, I was tempted to send this version. But then I thought of my editor, a family man and stalwart Republican, Knight of Columbus, and winner of countless Catholic Press awards. My confession would make him unhappy, and he wouldn't know what to do with it. He would confide in the managing editor, who would convince him that so unsavoury a character as I had no place in a Catholic media group, and I would be out of a job and probably back in Scotland within the month. So I erased the truth and wrote a passable piece of blarney that would have both flattered and alarmed the German bishops.

The buzzer sounded, and I let Suzy into the building. She came up the stairs, and I opened the door. Suzy had had her hair cut into a cute little bob and dyed scarlet. She was wearing a sweet little white dress over white lace leggings, and her red fingernails were perfectly manicured. A bicycle helmet hung from her wrist; she swung it nervously.

"Hi, Cat! Are you busy, or—?" She looked left and right along the hallway to see if anyone else was there.

"No, I'm not busy. Come in. Would you like a beer?"

"No, thank you. Coffee's fine."

"We don't have a regular coffeemaker, but I can make you a cappuccino."

"Thank you. That'll be great."

She took off her sandals and followed me into the kitchen.

I said, "I haven't seen you since Berlin."

Suzy sat at the wooden table and watched silently while I made her a cappuccino. After I set hers before her and turned to make my own, she cleared her throat and asked, "Did you get my email?"

There was a trace of exotic, Eastern scent in my kitchen, and I knew that Suzy was here to court Dennis. Her declaration hadn't been a cover or, as I'd wondered, a figment of my imagination. It was the real puppy-love deal. The hairdo, the manicure, the dress: all preparation for another heartfelt declaration. I wondered if Suzy had ever had a boyfriend at all.

"I got your email", I said. "The bombing rather shoved it into the back of my mind."

"The bombing?"

"The tube bombing in Berlin. A man was killed."

"Oh yes", said Suzy vaguely. "I heard about that. Well, I meant what I said. Whatever happens, I want us all to be friends."

"Sure", I said. "But I can't speak for Dennis. He hates being embarrassed."

"I'm not going to do anything embarrassing", said Suzy. "I'm just going to put everything on the table. I want to be honest and upfront.

I've told so many lies in my life and been such a faker, and I don't want to lie to either of you guys."

"You said that in Berlin", I said. "And yet you lied to me about why you went there."

Suzy was stunned. She stared at me. "What do you mean?"

"Berlin is activist heaven. You're one of the leaders of a student peace group. Dennis said you've got connections in the Palestinian Authority. So you weren't just there to tell me you fell in love with Dennis on the dance floor."

"You know about the PA stuff?"

"Of course. Dennis told me."

"But how would Dennis know?"

"He's a student, too. He hears all the Goethe-Uni gossip. And you're not exactly invisible, Suzanne. So why not come clean about Berlin?"

"I told you", said Suzy. "I was interested in the Pope protests. When I got to Berlin, I checked out the rally. It was awesome."

"Wasn't it? I didn't see you there."

"Well, I was there", she said stubbornly. "I left when the cops showed up. I didn't want to get deported."

"Do you know Magic?"

"I'm sorry?"

"He's in Antifa, an anarchist."

"I know a lot of people", said Suzy. "But I totally don't always remember their names. And I don't know a lot of anarchists personally. I don't believe in anarchy."

"What do you believe in?"

"I believe in peace", said Suzy. She looked out the window on her left. "The lilac bushes are really nice. I didn't know there were lilacs in Germany before I came."

"You sound homesick", I said.

"Sometimes", said Suzy. "It would be way easier if I could speak German. I don't get a lot of practice. My classes feel really slow, and some of the guys make it even slower by slacking off. It helps that so many people here speak English, but sometimes they forget that I can't understand them in German, and they just . . . I guess it saves time."

"You should speak to them only in German. That way you'll learn faster."

"That's what Aisha says. She says your German is only so good because of Dennis."

"Dennis' German would send my tutor reeling."

"You have a tutor?"

"I meant back at university. A university tutor is a kind of mentor."

Suzy pondered that. "I guess that's a British thing, then. What's wrong with Dennis' German?"

"Nothing, really. But he loves dialect words, and he picked up some ghastly expressions in the army."

"The *army*?" The word ended in a squeal of horror, and I enjoyed Suzy's expression of shock, the wide eyes, the slack jaw, the pretty red lips parted in dismay. I permitted myself to be amused.

"Well, of course. Germany has a draft, you know."

"But nobody actually goes into the army! They work for the social services instead."

"Only the 'pacifists'. And Dennis is certainly not a pacifist. In fact, in his younger days, he was quite a scrapper. He was hauled up for gay-bashing once; the judge ruled self-defense."

"Come on, you're joking", said Suzy. She seemed divided between amusement and distress. "No way! He's hardly that kind of guy."

"It was self-defense", I said, keeping my voice under control. "From Dennis' point of view anyway. He's been fending off advances since he was fourteen."

"You can defend yourself and still be a pacifist", said Suzy. "Why didn't he just say he was one?"

"Because he would have been lying. Dennis hates lying."

"Me, too. But some lies are necessary."

"Are they?"

Suzy wordlessly poked at the bottom of her cup with a spoon. Then I heard the street door open, and my heart sank. I had hoped Suzy would be gone before Dennis got home. There was his tread on the stairs, and Suzy froze.

"That's Dennis", she said as if she had heard him on the stairs before.

The door opened, and Dennis dropped his schoolbag in the hall-way with a thump. He looked into the kitchen. In German, he said, "They kicked us out of the library. They're cleaning the carpets this weekend." Then, in English, to Suzy, "Hello there."

"Dennis, you remember Suzy?" I said in English.

"Yes, of course", said Dennis. "The real Canadian."

"The real—?" Blushing, Suzy looked from Dennis to me.

"A private joke", I said. "He likes to say I got my Canadian passport in the black market. Anyway, Dennis, Suzy has something to say to you. Why don't we move to the sitting room and be comfortable?"

Dennis looked deeply suspicious. Suzy all but fled from the kitchen, clutching her helmet. Dennis went straight to the fridge and took out a beer.

"What's going on?" he asked.

I threw my hands up in the air, an imitation of my Scots grandmother, I realised, warding off blame.

"It's Suzy's thing", I said.

"Is it a rally?"

I sighed. "Don't worry. This can't take long."

I preceded him into the sitting room. Suzy sat bolt upright on the green leather couch. I sat in Dennis' favourite chair. That left him the striped chair, from which he gazed at both of us. Suzy, I was pleased to see, was suffering an agony of mortification. Her face was red, and her eyes were wide.

"This is, like, totally embarrassing", she muttered.

"Might as well get it over with then", I replied.

So she did. She explained to Dennis that she had come to Frankfurt only to learn German and organise a German branch of Peace Now. Strictly business. But then she had met Dennis, and she realised that there was more to life than school and peace activism. She explained the incident on the dance floor, and how she wanted to show Dennis a better life than that to be found in decadent parties in skyscrapers. She felt a great love for him, and she respected him very much as a man. She hoped that, after a period of getting to know each other better, he would consider marrying her.

It was an awful speech for a woman to give, and I blushed for her. Dennis, however, merely nodded thoughtfully through the whole, and it was clear to me, if not to Suzy, that he understood only about fifty percent of what she had said. In English, he asked if he might speak to me in German for a moment. Suzy nodded.

"Is she serious?" demanded Dennis.

"She sounds very serious to me. Did you get all that?"

"No. I don't understand about the club and the party."

I explained what she said about the club and the party.

70

"But I don't understand the point of all this", said Dennis. "Does she want me to join her group?"

"No, darling, she wants to marry you."

"What!"

"Dennis, it's not that hard to figure out. She came to Germany to start her little group. She met you. You smiled at her on the dance floor. She fell for you. Then she remembered that ghastly party and feared that you'd end up like Florian von Brandenburg zu Hessich. So she wants to marry you and presumably take you away to the pristine forests of Canada."

"Is she crazy?"

"I don't think so. Occasionally I have similar feelings myself."

"Well, what am I supposed to say?"

"Hey, it's a marriage proposal. Accept or reject."

Dennis looked at Suzy and coloured a little. Then he looked at me again and a smirk hovered at the corners of his mouth. "And what would you say if I accepted?"

I hesitated. Dennis was not given to emotional blackmail, but I didn't want there to be a first time. "I'd say what I always say. Twenty-two is too young to be married."

The smirk disappeared, and Dennis gave me an ice-blue look meant to freeze my blood. He turned his attention back to Suzy.

"Am I to understand that this is a proposal of marriage?" he asked in his fake Oxbridge voice.

"Um, yes. Sort of. I mean, you don't have to answer right away, eh?"

"It is a very flattering offer", said Dennis. "Thank you."

"I mean, I know you don't even know me. But, um, I'm a really good person, eh? I care about the world, and I believe men and women should contribute to the family, you know? If you want kids, as far as I know I can have them. And, um, I don't know if it's an issue, but I have money of my own. I mean, from my grandparents. They left it to me, in trust."

"A trust fund", I translated in a nasty tone. "She has old family money."

Dennis ignored me.

"I am flattered", he said.

"You're going to have to say more than that", I said *auf Deutsch*.

"Shut up", snarled Dennis. "Are you trying to get rid of me?"

"No."

"Are you leaving Germany?"

I thought of my promotion and said, "No."

"Then shut up. This is very embarrassing, and you're making it worse."

With what was perhaps an effort, he smiled at Suzy and said, "I am very happy that you think so well of me, but I have to say no."

"Okay", said Suzy.

It was as easy as that. She stood up. Her legs were a bit wobbly, I saw, but I didn't rejoice in it. I was merely relieved.

"No hard feelings, eh?" she said. "Still friends?"

"Still friends", said Dennis. He shook her hand.

Suzy laughed shakily.

Now that the ordeal was over, my feelings of intense dislike disappeared. "Come into the kitchen", I said. "Let's have a real chat. Girls only. No boys allowed."

"No, thank you", said Suzy. "I'd better go."

"You sure?"

"Yes, I'd better go. I need to clear my head."

"Well", said Dennis. "I'll see you later."

He went into the bedroom with his schoolbag and shut the door.

"I'll walk with you if you want."

"No, thanks, Cat. I need to be alone. I guess Dennis thinks I'm crazy, eh?"

"He'll think it's a cultural thing."

"A cultural thing?"

"You're Canadian. He'll put it down to that."

"We're not as boring as people say."

"Evidently not."

Suzy laughed and gently punched my arm. "You're all right, Cat. I wish you would marry him."

"I thought you were going to be honest with me."

"I am. If he doesn't marry me, well, he might as well marry you. I guess I just hate the thought of him being ruined. Ever since that party, I've been thinking about it."

"*The Portrait of Dorian Gray*", I said.

"The whatsit?"

"The concept of a man being 'ruined' is rather Gothic, but I think I know what you mean. Don't worry about it, Suzy. Despite all appearances to the contrary, Dennis has a wide moral streak."

"I know", said Suzy, and I suppressed the urge to push her down the stairs.

I saw her to the bottom and shut the door behind her. As I went up again, I wondered if the war was won or whether, once I was in Italy, news of Suzy's ultimate victory would reach me. She had very pretty legs.

Dennis was waiting for me when I walked back into the flat. He was furious. He came hurtling out of the bedroom and began shouting in the hall. When they are angry, German men make up for their considerable social restraint in the volume of their shouts. I, on the other hand, continue to speak in quiet, measured tones. It drives Dennis insane.

"How could you let her do it?"

"How could I stop her? You've seen what she's like."

"That was humiliating, for her and for me. And you, you just sat there, watching the whole thing as though it had nothing to do with you."

"It had nothing to do with me. I don't own you. You're a free man."

"Oh yes, completely free. We have a life together, remember? Why didn't you kick her out?"

"Is that what you wanted? A big jealous scene?"

"If it were the other way around—if it were Kurt or Michael—I would have thrown him down the stairs."

"Well, as a woman, I don't feel it necessary to prove myself by acting like a barbarian."

"The fact is", said Dennis, as if getting at the heart of the matter, "you don't love me."

"Dennis, let's not go through this again."

"If you loved me, you would marry me."

"I love you, so I don't marry you."

That caught him off guard, and he had to think for a moment. "That doesn't make any sense. Hannah says—"

"I don't give a damn about what Aisha says. Aisha doesn't have the slightest conception of what is good for you."

"And you do?"

"Yes", I said. "I do. And the first thing is that you are too young to get married. My ex-husband was twenty-two. So was I. And look what happened."

Dennis rolled his eyes, and I suppressed the urge to slap him.

"I am not your ex-husband", shouted Dennis in the exasperated tone of someone who has said it a hundred times before. "I am me, Deniz Erlichmann, and I know what I want in life, okay? I am not going to get bored of you and run off with some younger chicken. We have been together for two years. Why can't you trust me?"

"I do trust you. Look, if you were twenty-five, it would be different."

"*Scheisse*", roared Dennis. "You are not listening to me. You never listen to me. You always think you have the answer because you're older than me, because you're smarter than me. What do you think I am, some kind of toy? A child? A prize dog?"

"That's ridiculous."

"My parents say you'll never settle down if we keep just living together."

"What am I, a man? Women don't think that way, Dennis."

"Well then, Catriona, what is your problem?"

"What is your problem? You'd think this was the American South, not twenty-first-century Frankfurt. Most people just live together."

"That's a shitty argument. My family is religious. Your family is religious. Every time Uncle Franz mentions me, both my parents have heart attacks."

"Then leave. Go home."

Dennis gave me another of his ice-blue looks, and I shivered.

"Do you want me to leave?" he asked. "Because if you do, I will. I'm tired of this crap about my age. And I'm tired of your guilt. Your guilt makes me feel guilty, and I hate that. So what is the story?"

I considered bluffing for about five seconds. "I don't want you to leave."

Dennis looked triumphant.

"Good", he said. "Then you'd better marry me or I *will* leave. There."

"But I can't", I groaned. "Your people—and my people—will kill me if there's no church wedding, and, Dennis, I lied. I am leaving Germany. I'm being sent to Rome. To Vatican City. They want me to be bureau chief."

Dennis stalked into the kitchen, and after a frightened moment, I followed. He was slumped in a chair at the table, his arms crossed.

"But you're not going, right?"

"If I don't, what are we going to live on? They don't want a German correspondent anymore. They'll fire me."

"Then I'll come with you. We'll get married, and we'll live in Rome. I like Rome."

"You have school, and I can't get married in the Church yet, anyway."

"Always the excuses", said Dennis bitterly. "We could get married in the Rathaus now and in church later. I'll go to lectures at the Gregorian. I'll find a job. There's nothing to stop us."

"Except Uncle Franz."

Dennis said something very rude and unnecessary about Uncle Franz. He got up, shoved the chair under the table, and stood at the window, staring at the lilac bushes Suzy had so admired. And perhaps it was this reminder of Suzy—and of all the other women prowling outside our relationship like jackals—that tipped the balance. I heard myself saying, "Dennis, when I get my annulment—and I don't know when that will be—I will marry you. Just don't . . . leave."

Dennis didn't turn around, but he visibly relaxed. "Swear?"

"Swear."

"Even if it comes next week?"

"Even if it comes next week."

"Good", said Dennis. He went out of the kitchen and came back with a box. The box contained a ring with what was among the jeweller's smallest diamonds. It was the kind of ring appropriate to the fiancée of a philosophy student/clerk in the Hauptbahnhof bookstore. I put it on. Dennis called his parents.

The letter announcing that my first marriage was null and void arrived two weeks after that. The post came late; Dennis was at school. I wasn't sure what to do with it. In the end, I hid it in my underwear drawer and said nothing about it to anyone.

Chapter 2

Once every few years, the Temple Dance Priest takes his show back on the European road, and although he was concentrating on the Slavic nations, this time he wangled a few invitations to eastern Germany. He was a figure of fun back in the New York office, the symbol of everything wrong and decadent in the Church today, so my editor, promising to address soon my email about leaving Germany, sent me to Dresden to interview him.

It was a blazing hot day, and the semi-rural suburb in which Saint Matilda's Seminary rests was no cooler than the city centre. I remembered the modern chapel, shaped like an egg or a tomb, to be a cool, bare, quiet place. But on that day even the chapel was filled with a dry heat. It was made worse by the crush of seminarians—ordered to attend—and the sight of the altar servers in their thick white albs, silently sweating. The only figures truly dressed for the weather were the metal statue of Krishna standing before the altar and the Temple Dance Priest himself.

He, a lean, brown, and wiry figure, was wearing only white breeches with a short skirt and a gold stole that covered his nipples. He was wearing lashings of jewellery, including earrings, and more paint than a Sankt Pauli prostitute. At the beginning of Mass, he sat composedly while the celebrant explained how the liturgy would unfold, and after the Gospel reading, got up and introduced his first dance in English. His voice was unusually high and flutelike. His German translator, a pinched blonde woman in a blue sari, struggled to keep up with him, but he seemed to ignore her. Then he switched on his portable cassette player, and Hindi music erupted into the chapel.

I enjoy Indian dance, but I did not know that Indian men could dance as do the women: batting their lashes, rolling their eyes, and making delicate gestures with their hands. Macho American journalists in Frankfurt often made fun of the theatrics of "injured" footballers;

I wondered what they would think of the Temple Dance Priest. The contrast between the bare grey chapel and the little brown man in eyeliner, smiling, winking, and dancing, was ludicrous. The Germans—seminarians, professors, and female lay students—looked pale and stone-faced, utterly inscrutable, even to me. Droplets of sweat ran down the altar servers' faces.

The second dance was in place of the offertory hymn, and the Temple Dance Priest informed us, over his companion's translation, that in this dance he would be the woman who wept over and perfumed Jesus' feet and wiped them with her hair. Now the music sounded intensely erotic, and I wondered if it was quite fair to the gay men and to the women in the chapel to have to watch a half-naked man dance through Mass. I tried to catch the eye of a handsome seminarian on the right side of the chapel, but to no avail. Blond and high-nosed, he gazed on as still and solemn as a marble statue. I looked back at the Temple Dance Priest and thought about Dennis. I wasn't going up for Communion anyway.

The gold stole came off for the dance that followed Holy Communion, but this time I was neither shocked nor titillated but merely bored. The dance went on much too long, and I felt sorry, even angry, for the German priests and altar servers in their heavy cream robes. I never feel at ease in Dresden as it is. Only there does the West German miasma of shared guilt affect me. When I visit, I avoid speaking English as much as possible.

When Mass was over, the Temple Dance Priest sat back on his pew and vigorously towelled himself. I introduced myself to the translator and asked if I might interview the cleric through her. She frowned at the idea and was sure Father Francis would prefer to speak with me in English. Her frown deepened when I pointed out that we were all in Germany, as if I had insulted her cosmopolitan, sari-clad nature. In the end, we approached the Temple Dance Priest together, and she explained in English who I was. I handed him my business card, and his eyebrows knit together over his painted eyes. I hoped he recognised the name of the newsgroup without remembering what they had previously said about him.

"What would you like to know?" he asked in his feminine voice.

"Well, Father Francis, first I would like to know about your training. Who were your teachers?"

He relaxed a little.

"I was formed by a phalanx of phenomenal gurus", he said dreamily. "All the greatest teachers of the Bharatanatyam tradition in this and the latter half of the previous century. And there are others too many to mention; you can look up my website."

"And your theological training?"

Father Francis looked suspicious again and turned his face away.

"Just a minute. Does Father Kaefer want to speak to me?" he snapped at his translator. She fluttered forward and drew a grey-headed priest into conversation with her. The dancer turned his gaze to me again. "Well, of course, I was educated at the seminary in Mumbai. But obviously my mission is to bridge cultures and religion through dance, and there was not much of an opportunity to do that in the seminary."

"It might be controversial", I said, "bringing Krishna into a Christian worship space."

"Controversial?" asked the Temple Dance Priest. His bejewelled hands fluttered. "How do you mean? Krishna is a cultural manifestation of God. You know, Christianity in India. . . . It is not like here, a Christian country, where Christianity is natural to the environment. It was stifled, you see, hemmed in by a foreign, Western view. Obsessed with dogma. Conservative. It is my mission to bring the Church into mainstream Indian culture."

"And vice versa?"

"What's that?"

"Well, today you have brought mainstream Indian culture into a German Catholic church."

"Yes, exactly", said Father Francis. "It amazes me that the Church has ignored dance—such an important medium of culture—for so long. And Krishna is, you might say, the ultimate expression of Indian culture."

"Many would say that dance is not part of the Christian liturgical tradition."

"King David danced. And, of course, so did Jesuit ballet masters of the European Renaissance. What I do is take traditional temple dance, dance that is sacred to the gods, to Shiva, to Krishna, and use it to express my commitment to Jesus."

"I see", I said, wiping my hot forehead. "The South-Asian population of Germany is growing. Do you have any concerns or thoughts about the growing xenophobia here in Saxony?"

The Temple Dance Priest looked away again toward Father Kaefer. "Does he want me?" he demanded. He rose. "I'm sorry. Perhaps if you were to call my mobile I could give you a longer interview. The number is on the back of my programme. You see there." He pointed to the Mass booklet in my hands.

I thanked him, and he went out of the chapel with his blonde translator and the tall, grey priest, following the straggling students. I collared one of the altar servers, coming out from behind the sacristy hidden in the back. He was now dressed in beige cotton trousers and a football jersey.

"I didn't mind his costume", said the boy, taking off his glasses to wipe the sweat from his nose. "It was the idol. I don't understand what it was doing in the chapel. Maybe if he had left it outside the chapel, or maybe at the back. Me, I couldn't tell who he was dancing for."

"David danced before the Lord", I quoted.

"Yeah," laughed the seminarian, "but *our* Lord."

"You don't think Krishna a cultural manifestation of our Lord?"

"No", said the seminarian. "But don't tell Father Kaefer I said so."

I went outside under the shade of the huge oak trees sheltering the entrance to the seminary, and saw Suzy sitting on a bench, talking to the handsome blond boy who had caught my eye. Her hair had faded to a fiery orange, and her roots were dark. She bounced up when I called, and I saw that she had a flower stud in her nose. My thoughts flew to my engagement ring, hanging from a gold chain under my blouse. I wondered if Aisha had told her yet.

"You should have come inside", I said. "You would have liked the jewellery."

"No way!" said Suzy, rolling her eyes. "I totally did, and then I went right back out again. I like men who are men, know what I mean? This is Norbert."

"Hello, Norbert", I said. "Are you one of Suzy's peaceniks?"

Norbert smiled. It was a nice shy smile. "We just met", he said.

"Norbert saw me sitting there and came over to say hi. Wasn't that nice?"

"Very nice", I said. "What are you doing here?"

"Oh, Dennis said you would be here. I was at TU-Dresden, giving a presentation for Peace Now."

I laughed. "I don't know how you do it all without any German."

"Hey", shouted Suzy, grinning. "I'm the best in my class. I can tell you when my head is hurting, and when my feet are hurting, and when my teeth are hurting. If I ever have to go to a German doctor, I'm all set. Come and see my car. I'll drive you back to Frankfurt, if you're done."

"How did you get a car?"

"One of my buddies rented it for me."

"I was going to take the train", I said. I wondered if I had enough energy to bear four hours of Suzy. Still, I needed someone to clear my soul of Father Francis' gyrations, and I wasn't looking forward to waiting for the bus to the Hauptbahnhof.

"Come on", said Suzy. "It's air-conditioned."

"First come and see the campus", said Norbert. He was obviously taken with Suzy. I liked that.

"Okay", said Suzy. "Cool! But not too long. I need to get back before six."

"You kids go on ahead", I said. "I've seen it, and I'm too hot to move."

"You could get a drink in the Mensa", said Norbert. "It's open until three."

A breeze had stirred up, and the wall-length windows of the cafeteria had been thrown open to meet it. It was a pretty dining room, not at all institutional, with white walls, pale wooden tables and chairs, and a skylight. The plastic gerberas on each table looked real, but they were rooted in little blue bottles filled with sand. I bought a litre of mineral water and sat at a window with a view of the woods. The students around me chatted amiably about their studies and social lives as they ate their huge and meaty midday meal or smoked. The heat had taken away my appetite.

I looked at the woods and random memories fluttered through my mind like birds: my ex-husband on the banks of the Cam, quarrelling with a friend about the *Nicomachean Ethics* while I sunbathed; my Canadian grandmother mixing up orange juice from a packet of powder; the puppy that cried under our window until Dennis went out to free him from the fence; my ex-husband telling me, in his blunt way, that I was bad in bed and a bore and that he had found someone else. I thought of the annulment decree in my underwear drawer and wondered if my ex-husband had already married his girlfriend. She had been his student, the last of a long line of student-girlfriends. He was, I thought, taking quite a risk. In ten years, he might find her a bore, too. It would have been smarter to wait until he was over forty. A twenty-year gap renders a wife young forever. I watched as Norbert and Suzy emerged from the glass cube where classes were held and walked toward the Mensa. Suzy waved, and I put the blue cap back on my water bottle.

We said our good-byes to Norbert, and Suzy led me to a black Audi in the parking lot behind the chapel.

"That's a good-looking bloke", said I to Suzy.

"Ah", said Suzy dismissively. "Not my type. There sure are a lot of blond men in this country. They remind me of little kids."

"I know Germans who think all North Americans are like little kids."

"Ha", said Suzy, starting up the air conditioner. "They should talk."

* * *

As we distanced ourselves from Dresden, my inherited war guilt slipped away to make room for apprehension. Unemployment was high in Saxony, and this had brought anger, xenophobia, and votes for far-right parties. Dennis, who was otherwise apolitical, called the area "Nazi land" and got upset if I drove through it alone.

"Did you fill up with petrol in Dresden?" I asked casually.

Suzy hadn't, but she did have three-quarters of a tank. "I figure there'll be a service station along if we need it", she said. "Don't you?"

"I think we should wait until we get to a bigger town. Weimar, for example."

Suzy looked surprised. "Oh, . . . Do you think someone would hassle us? I mean, we're white, right?"

"Not white enough for the NPD—Nationaldemokratische Partei Deutschlands, I mean. We're still foreigners."

"Well, I guess I'd keep my mouth shut, and let you do the talking", said Suzy. She sighed, "Racism really sucks."

"Indeed."

"Did you know that there is no racism in Islam?"

"Pass that along to the Saudis", I said.

"What do you mean?"

"They treat Pakistani migrants like the dust under their sandals, and their word for a black person is synonymous with 'slave'."

"No", said Suzy, deeply shocked. "That can't be right."

"Well, don't take it from me. Ask Aisha when you see her."

81

Suzy was quiet.

"How's Dennis?" she asked. "Is he well?"

"When he's not stoned or hung over, he's always well."

"Stoned! He uses drugs?"

"Just weed", I said. "Once in a while, if he's feeling anxious. I'll thank you not to share that information with his sister."

There was another uncharacteristic silence, and then Suzy said, "I saw Aisha yesterday."

"Did she invite you over for dinner?"

"She did, but I couldn't go."

"She doesn't give up, does she?"

"Give up on what?"

"I think she thinks you'd make a better sister-in-law."

"She says you're leaving Germany."

"Wishful thinking."

Suzy said, "You'd tell me if you were, Cat, wouldn't you? You wouldn't, you know, screw me over?"

"What do you mean?"

"I mean, you wouldn't just ditch Dennis without telling me? Because I'm leaving, and I wouldn't want him to be left in Frankfurt without either of us."

This was certainly news to me.

"Dennis is capable of taking care of himself without female aid", I said. "Why are you leaving?"

"I couldn't take it", said Suzy simply. "I just keep thinking about him all the time. I need to go somewhere else."

"When are you going?"

"In December. I've applied to join an aid group in Pakistan."

"But what about Peace Now? You seem to be its heart and soul."

"They'll be fine without me", said Suzy. "My job is just to set it up."

"Did you tell the others why?"

"I told the other team leaders: Mike and Sean, Lukas and Julia. You met them at the KK, remember?"

"I suppose they think I'm a real bitch for not letting you run off with my too-young-for-me boyfriend."

"Well, Mike and Sean, sort of, but Lukas and Julia were totally on your side."

The engine was making banging noises. They may have been going on for some time before I noticed it, for I was wholly absorbed in

Suzy's question, "You wouldn't screw me over?" It suggested that we had some kind of obligation to each other. What, in Suzy's mind, was it based on? Shared citizenship or the mutual accident of having been born female? But I supposed it might have stemmed from being in love with the same man, for that was how Suzy's mind worked. In her shoes, I would have hated me for sleeping with the man I wanted. Instead, Suzy seemed to admire me for it, as though I were the richest, most popular girl in her school.

"What the hell is that?" asked Suzy.

I woke up to the banging sounds. "I have no idea."

The engine continued its banging, and Suzy turned quite pale.

"I'll pull over", she said.

We stared at the engine with mutual incomprehension.

"I wish Dennis were here", I muttered.

"Oh! Does he understand cars?"

"He loves cars. Go wave down a German."

"Are you sure? I mean, you said ... What about the neo-Nazis?"

"Even a neo-Nazi is unlikely to hurt a car if he's German."

Suzy waved down a German who was not a neo-Nazi but a salesman on his way to Leipzig. He looked into the engine with great interest and explained that the problem was the fan belt. It was coming apart. Indeed, it was going to snap entirely. The battery would probably see us through to the next town, though. He recommended we turn off at the next exit.

We were in luck. The engine lasted until we were thirty yards from a service station. It was in a little town, very pretty, though crumbling from sixty years of socialist neglect. It did not seem to have suffered much war damage. At the same time, it was saved from an unreal Disney air by the modern shopwindows, occasional graffiti, and stickers littering the lampposts. The streets, though, were unnaturally empty.

I told Suzy to stay in the car and went into the service station to explain our predicament. The burly, middle-aged owner looked out the door at the stalled Audi and called to his sons in the garage. The sons wiped their hands on rags and went out to push the car down the street to the shop.

The owner had a salt-and-pepper moustache. He rubbed it thoughtfully. "Where do you come from?" he asked.

"I? From Frankfurt."

"That is, where have you driven from today?"

"From Dresden."

"Ah", said the owner. "Bad news there today."

He gestured to the television on his desk, and turned it around so I could see. A reporter I didn't know was standing in front of the Dresden Hauptbahnhof, talking to an agitated woman whose bag strap kept slipping from her shoulder. There had been an explosion.

"A construction accident?" I asked.

"*Tja.* It was no accident. It was a bomb."

"But the station hasn't even been finished yet", I wanted to say. The heat was making me stupid. Instead I asked if anyone had claimed responsibility.

"Not yet. But it doesn't matter. We know who it is, don't we?"

I forced myself to meet the owner's gaze and heard myself say, "Foreigners?" My mind stood back and applauded my performance.

"Exactly", said the old man. "That's all we need to know, Miss."

*   *   *

I took Suzy away to a clean-looking and, above all, empty restaurant.

"Don't even open your mouth when someone approaches", I told her. "If someone speaks to you, pretend you're deaf."

"What's wrong?"

"Somebody bombed the Dresden Hauptbahnhof."

Suzy's eyes widened. "What? When? That's terrible! You could have been killed!"

"Some people were killed. The police aren't saying how many."

"Shouldn't you call Dennis? He must be freaking!"

I called Dennis; he didn't answer. Feeling aggrieved, I left a message as the waitress approached. I did a double-take: she was a foreigner, Turkish or Bosnian perhaps. I wondered what life here was like for her. The menu was limited; I ordered a salad and juice for Suzy, and a gin and tonic for me. I felt I had earned it.

"Why did they do it?" asked Suzy. "Afghanistan?"

"Does it matter? They did it, that's all. If they wanted to kill Germans, they did. End of story."

In her excitement, Suzy missed the warning in my tone. "This wouldn't have happened if Germany weren't in Afghanistan. The German government is endangering the lives of its people."

"Save it for the university kids", I said. "The Chancellor didn't build that bomb."

84

"Oh, but she totally did, morally speaking", said Suzy.

"Suzy", I said. "You're a nice girl, but I'm only going to say this once. Shut up."

Suzy turned red and shut up. The waitress brought my gin and tonic and Suzy's juice. She seemed nervous; her hand shook a little as she set our frosty glasses on the table. A question seemed to hover on her lips. Then the door slammed open, and a dark-haired young man appeared in the restaurant, shouting instructions in a language I didn't know. The waitress shrieked and rushed into the kitchen. From the street, I could hear yelling and the strains of martial music. Glass smashed. I choked on my drink and rose to my feet.

"What is it?" demanded Suzy.

"Skinheads", I said. "We're for it."

The young man stared at us, considering for a moment, and then jerked his thumb toward the door. He said in German, "You, out!"

"*Bitte*", I said. "We are also foreigners."

The young man hesitated and then nodded. I grabbed Suzy's hand and pulled her with me into the kitchen. I looked for the waitress and saw her disappearing down cellar stairs. We followed after, scrambling down the long, winding staircase in the dim light. The waitress scurried down a passage, and we scurried after. She came to a metal door and knocked on it. The door opened, and looking back, she held it open for us. We went in and felt several pairs of eyes turn in our direction. There was an old man, and a young man of perhaps seventeen. There was an old woman in a hijab, a younger woman in a hijab, and three children of varying ages. They were seated on cots and battered chairs about the lamplit room, battered suitcases open or shut along the floor. So another family might have sat over sixty years before as British bombs rained down upon Dresden. I wondered how long this one had been there and what their final destination would be. Frankfurt? Berlin? Glasgow? New York?

Beside me Suzy nodded her head. "*Salaam Alaikum*", she said.

The dark eyes stared back, unblinking. We advanced slowly into the room and sat on a legless, brown, velour couch. A terrible crunching, smashing sound came from far above. The children screamed and ran to their mother, who was sitting on a cot. She put her arms around them. The children wept silently; I suppose they had been trained to. The old woman began moaning. The younger woman spoke soothingly to her, but the old woman skirled, "O Allah, Allah, Allah, Allah."

There was hammering of feet on the iron staircase, and the waitress opened the door. The young man burst in. His hands were bleeding. I wondered if he had managed to shut the metal siding in time, but from the sounds above, I decided not. The waitress slammed and bolted the door behind him, and then took his hands in hers and examined them. They had a strong family resemblance; I decided that they must be brother and sister.

Suzy turned and looked at me, her face ghastly in the dim light. "What do we do?" she asked.

"Do? Nothing. We wait it out."

"Will the police come?"

"The last thing this lot wants to see is the police."

The sounds of fierce merrymaking, if you could call it that, continued unabated. The martial music and the smashing drifted downstairs. The waitress and her brother sat separately from the family, and I decided that they were unrelated, merely the stationmasters at this stop on the underground immigration railway.

I took out my pack of diplomatic cigarettes, and both the waitress and her brother took one with brief thanks. The old man showed an interest, so I went over and offered one to him, too. He took one and sat back in his chair. Meanwhile, Suzy went over to the old lady and tried to comfort her with her rudimentary Turkish or Arabic. I was glad; I was unsure as to whether the waitress and her brother were regretting our rescue. I was relatively sure the Nazis wouldn't cut our throats; I couldn't say the same for the smugglers. We might need to be rescued by the smuggled.

As if reading my thoughts, the young man spoke up in a low voice. "Where do you come from?"

"From Scotland", I said.

"And she?"

"Canada."

"What are you doing in Germany?"

"I am a journalist", I said. "I have an office in Frankfurt." I added a useful lie. "My editor will wonder why I'm not back yet."

"*Klar*", said the young man. The waitress touched his arm, and they had a quiet conversation together.

The young man addressed me again. "Why are you here in Saxony?"

"Our car broke down", I said. Above us, something heavy fell to the floor. "I hope you have insurance."

He ignored that. Suzy came back and sat beside me. The men above had begun to sing loud and unpleasant songs. I was glad Suzy couldn't understand them, and I hoped the émigrés couldn't either.

"How long will they stay up there?" she asked.

"Until they run out of booze."

"Animals", said Suzy. "You talk about terrorists. They're the *real* terrorists."

"Hardly", I said. "From their point of view, they're freedom fighters. Patriots."

"That's disgusting. How can you say that?"

"Because I've been in Pakistan. Lebanon. Jerusalem. Paris. I've hidden from mobs before. And I don't believe in double standards. So the neo-Nazis march through the streets yelling death to foreigners and Jews? So do Palestinians and their friends. Only they don't confine it to Palestine. They do it through the streets of Paris and London. New York, even. Toronto. Montreal. In America, they have the sense to stick to Arabic and Urdu when they yell. Why are we supposed to hold Europeans to a higher standard than Asians? At least they're at home."

Suzy shifted. "Sometimes I hate the way you talk, Cat. It sounds racist to me."

"It's the opposite of racist. One rule for everyone. Nobody should be allowed to get away with yelling 'Death to the Jews.' Nobody should be allowed to harass foreigners, or call them dirty or disgusting. Mecca's off-limits to unbelievers, but it wasn't so holy that it couldn't be bulldozed to make room for hotels."

"Anyway," said Suzy, "Muslims are Semites, too."

I didn't see how that followed, but I left it alone.

A bottle smashed. Raucous laughter followed.

"It's like Kristelnacht all over again", said Suzy.

"Hardly. No one's going to blame the Jews for the Dresden bomb. Except some Muslims and some mental professors in America."

"Muslims are the new Jews", said Suzy.

"In most places, Jews are the new Jews", I said. "Haven't you noticed?"

There was a loud splintering noise, as if a chair had been smashed against the bar. Suzy winced.

"Let's not fight about it. It's bad enough what's going on upstairs."

"A home invasion. A gang of thugs having a good time."

"But, Catriona, they're *neo-Nazis*."

"Would it be any different if they weren't?"

"Yes", cried Suzy. "They're the scum of the earth!"

"There's a number of contenders for that title. Neo-Nazis didn't blow up the Twin Towers."

"That's different. That was a blow against American imperialism."

"Nice talk for a pacifist."

"I mean from their point of view", said Suzy, blushing. "I guess it really comes down to point of view, doesn't it?"

"Does it? I think it comes down to people hiding in cellars and glass in the street. People of any colour being blown to bits as they go about the difficult business of living."

"So you *are* a pacifist", said Suzy.

"I'm no pacifist", I said. "I'm just nostalgic for the trenches. Honour in clean battle may have been a myth, but at least there was a myth. Those Americans who fought back on 9/11, who tried to take control of the plane, they believed the myth. Now they're part of the myth. Maybe I've been too hard on Antifa. At least they put their own bodies on the line. Bombers don't—unless they think they'll get a heavenly reward for it. And Antifa doesn't."

I wondered where they were. In my experience, neo-Nazi demonstrations were always outnumbered and checked by busloads of anti-Nazis. Perhaps this was a sudden uprising, inspired by the bombing. Or perhaps Dennis was right, and some eastern villages were effectively controlled by the NPD. I hoped not. Despite the embarrassment their arrival would cause our rescuers, I was counting on the police.

"Don't you believe in any cause?" asked Suzy, almost wistfully.

"Not causes, unless Catholicism is a cause."

"You're a funny kind of Catholic, aren't you, Cat?"

"Aisha thinks I'm typical. So do I. I've just had a better theological education than most, and therefore fewer excuses. Here, offer the others more cigarettes."

When Suzy came back, I said, "I hope that bought a little more friendship."

"Don't you trust them?"

"We're not awfully convenient. We're worth nothing as hostages, and we've stumbled on a smuggling operation. We might make good decoys, though. I keep thinking about Lot's daughters."

"They wouldn't kick us out, would they?"

"They might. They might not. Fortunately, we're women, and there are children around. People usually behave better when there are children involved."

Suzy was quiet. I listened to the singing upstairs.

"Germans don't seem to like children", said Suzy. "Even Aisha doesn't have any."

"I think it's the taxes", I said. "And the women stay in school longer and then go out to work. There aren't a lot of incentives."

"Children themselves should be incentives", said Suzy. "I think Tarkan and Aisha would be happier if they had children."

"I didn't know they were unhappy."

"Well", said Suzy. "Do you want children, Cat?"

"Sometimes I think I do."

"I do", said Suzy. "That's why I care so much that we have a better world. I want a world in which all men and women really are brothers and sisters. Where people put aside their own selfishness to really live as God wants them to, you know? I don't believe in the separation of government and religion. I just think everyone should have to obey the laws of God. Children will only be safe in a world like that."

"I suppose that depends on what the laws are."

"I guess that's kind of a shocking to say, since back home we talk so much about the separation of church and state. But I didn't realise what that really meant until I came to Europe. People here really hate religion. And they're completely obsessed with sex. There's porn everywhere—have you noticed? On TV, in the ads, even kids' magazines. And the men act like beauty queens—they care so much about their hair and their clothes. They even use skin products. It's weird. And Silke says that German men are, um, funny in bed."

Suzy's voice dropped to a murmur. I could well imagine that Silke's lovers were funny in bed, but I asked, "Really? How?"

"She didn't say."

"That's too bad", I said. "My experience in that department is limited to one."

Suzy flinched but hurried on. "Anyway," she said, "it's not healthy. All this sex saturation makes men bored with normal sex. I think religious people are right to wait until marriage. That way sex is still special, you know?"

"Not really", I said. "When I was married, sex wasn't particularly special."

"Maybe you were married to the wrong man", said Suzy.

"That much is certain. Keep an eye on our pal over there. I'm going to have a look around."

I had noticed that beyond the cot where the old lady was still rocking and muttering to herself there was a passage to somewhere else. It occurred to me that there might be a way out of the building from the cellar, even if just a window. I am tall but narrow, and Suzy was a slim girl. I gave the package of cigarettes to Suzy and got up. The waitress and her brother looked alarmed.

"Where are you going?" demanded the brother.

"To the toilet", I said. "I imagine there must be one down here."

"Okay", he said. "But leave your phone here."

My phone didn't work underground anyway, so I agreed and left it with Suzy. I squeezed around the old lady's cot and felt my way along the passage wall. It was damp and dank. When my hand met empty air, I flicked on my lighter. There was the toilet and a sink. I continued to walk carefully, hand on the wall. Then I came to another chamber, and I held my breath for fear that I would walk into another band of refugees. I listened but heard nothing but the sounds of the brutal revelry above. Slowly I walked along the perimeter of the room, and then down a third passage. Eventually I saw a chink of light. There was a window, and there, up a short flight of wooden steps, was a door. It was bolted shut, and the bolt was leprous with rust. I gripped its curved end and tugged. The bolt didn't move. The metal hurt my fingers. I wiped them on my shirt and tried again. This time the bolt gave a few millimeters before the skin rubbed off my knuckles. I swore. Still, it looked promising. I decided to go back before our rescuers came looking for me.

When I returned, the scene was the same. Our rescuers were sitting on wooden chairs on either side of the metal door. The old man was in his chair. The teenage boy was leaning on the wall, listlessly drawing patterns in the dust with his shoe. The mother was curled over her children. The smallest had cried herself to sleep in her lap. The others looked glassy-eyed. The old lady was passing worry beads through her fingers. For the life of me, I could not guess their nationality. Neither the old man nor the teenage boy had shaved for at least a week, so that gave me no clue. They might have been Turks, or they

90

might have been fair-skinned Pakistanis, or Afghans, or Iraqis. I sat down on the legless couch beside Suzy.

"Don't show any emotion", I said. "I may have found a way out."

"Do you think it would be safer outside?"

"I think it might become so. But I don't know what's on the other side of the door."

"You don't seem scared", said Suzy.

"I'm frightened almost out of my wits. But that door looks very solid, and we've now got an escape plan."

"I wouldn't want to leave the kids."

"There's nothing we can do for the kids. Leave them to Brother and Sister over there. I'll bet Brother has a gun."

"You think?"

"You would need one in his racket. Just relax for now. Nap if you can. I'm going to try myself."

"Do you think that's safe?"

"Brother and Sister will be fine so long as the Nazis don't find us." I closed my eyes and tried to imagine myself somewhere else—at the day spa outside Cambridge, having a massage, preparatory to having my nails done, my hair done. I used to frequent it when my books were becoming popular, and money was rolling in. My husband hadn't found me boring yet. In those days, I was happy to be a standing stone, gathering moss. I had not yet had my moss ripped away, nor begun to roll hither and thither for fear of gathering moss again. But then I had rolled to a stop in Frankfurt, having bumped into Dennis, and he had taken root.

It was now close to four. Dennis would be at work at the station bookshop; in response to the Dresden bombing, there would be police all over the Hauptbahnhof. I wondered if my editor had responded to my email about staying in Frankfurt yet. I hoped not. The longer he took to make up his mind, the longer I could put off the inevitable.

Suzy was huddled in the corner of the couch, with her head on the arm.

"Are you asleep?" I asked.

"No."

"What are you thinking about."

She hesitated. "Dennis", she said.

"Ah."

"I wonder what he's doing now."

"I can tell you that. He's at the Hauptbahnhof bookshop, attending to the beginning of rush hour. He's checked his messages, and, in quiet moments, he is wondering why I'm not answering my mobile. He's annoyed that I am on the road, not flying like a reasonable person. But he's also checking his phone for texts from Kurt or Michael to see when they're meeting tonight. They're not sure if they want to go to KK's or a new place. Maybe they'll all end up in our flat, eating what they call Chinese food and playing video games. Maybe they'll go out, and Dennis will keep checking his phone."

"How nice to know", said Suzy, wistfully. "You're so lucky. Dennis must care for you so much."

"He hasn't had a chance to get bored yet", I said.

"You're so cynical", said Suzy. "I'm sure Dennis isn't like that. To me, he seems like a hero, you know. Like in a book, where the guy wants to be something great, but there are so many temptations in the way."

"My hero", I said, hating her, hating myself. "Saint Dennis of Frankfurt-am-Main, patron saint of clubbers and hair gel."

"Where did you meet him?"

"At his uncle's installation."

"Installation? You mean, an art show?"

"No, I mean when his great-uncle was made Archbishop of Kleinburg. I was reporting on it; Dennis kidnapped me and took me to a club."

"That sounds so romantic", said Suzy. "You've had so much romance in your life, Cat."

"I'm in my thirties. When you're as old as I am, you'll have had a lot of romance too."

"I don't know", said Suzy. "I've never had a boyfriend."

"Well, from many perspectives, that's a good thing. I bet Aisha wished she could have said that when she married Tarkan."

"Oh", said Suzy, blushing. "I didn't just mean serious boyfriends. I mean *any* boyfriend. I've never had one, and I've never told anybody."

"You're only twenty-two. It's not a big deal."

"Did you have a lot of boyfriends, growing up?"

"Not really."

"You think it is stupid to date a lot of people?"

"It's a waste of time, energy, and hope. And chasing men coarsens the soul. The sex feminists sold us a bill of goods, Suzy. Better to be a violet by a mossy stone beside the springs of Dove."

"You don't think I'm always going to be alone, do you?"

"Most people get married—and you're only twenty-two. Don't gauge your attractiveness by how many German guys ask you out. They won't. Young Germans are like us British: they wander around in packs."

"Sometimes I want sex so bad, I can barely sleep", said Suzy in a low voice.

"It gets better as you get older. If I didn't have Dennis, I'd be fine. I just wouldn't think about it."

"But you have Dennis", muttered Suzy.

"Trying to get sex outside of a relationship is one of the stupider things women do", I said. "Most men can get their kicks and wander off without turning a hair. Most women can't. That's something else the sex feminists don't tell you. Stay as you are. The right guy will come along. I bet Aisha could set you up with someone, since you're all fired up about Islam."

"I bet you think I'm kind of crazy for just wanting to get married and have babies."

"No, I think most women do—or did until they were told it was shameful. I think it's the most natural thing in the world."

"Wow, you know, Cat, it's really great talking to you like this. I've always wanted to, but I was kind of scared. You're just so much more sophisticated and stuff. You wrote a book in German, and you know all kinds of things I don't."

"There's nothing like a crisis for bringing people together. Tomorrow you'll hate me for listening to your secrets."

"As if. What was the most romantic moment in your life?"

I thought back. "I was on a flight from Edinburgh to London, and I was late. My luggage was the last to make it onto the carousel. There was trouble on the line; my train was delayed. When I got out at Paddington, I was so cross and tired, I could barely stand myself. And there, on the street, all in black, was a man with an umbrella, waiting for me. And I realised that it was that man that I had been trying to get to all that time."

"Was that Dennis?"

"No", I said. "It was someone before him."

"What happened?

"Well, nothing happened, really. He was a priest."

"What!"

"It happens. Priests are men. Et cetera."

93

"That is so totally shocking", said Suzy and I could see that for the moment she had forgotten the skinheads rampaging upstairs. "How could you?"

"You're more Catholic than you think. If we were Islamic, there wouldn't have been a problem."

"That's true", said Suzy. "Forcing men to stay celibate is seriously cruel."

"He wasn't forced. You might as well say that respecting your marriage vows to a wife you love is cruel. But our attempts at just being friends were driving us both crazy, so in the end I went away. I went to Frankfurt."

"And found Dennis."

"Well, to be fair, he found me."

"If you're so religious, why didn't you marry him then?"

"A twenty-year-old?"

"Well, then why didn't you keep away from him? You kept away from that priest."

"Dennis was a lot worse behaved than the priest. The priest was my age, and a good, honourable Irishman, freckled and modest, full of integrity. But Dennis was a conniving young wretch, who wanted what he wanted, and schemed to get it. And whenever he was around, my brain fogged up. It makes you wonder about Cassandra, why on earth she didn't give into Apollo."

"Who?"

"It's just an old story. But maybe Cassandra was right. You give in to the gods at your peril. Look at Leda. Sorry—another old story."

"If you don't marry him, you might lose him", said Suzy wisely.

"My dear Suzy, if I did marry him, I might lose him anyway. What is marriage anyway, in this day and age?"

"It's a covenant", said Suzy.

"What?" I stared at her. It was if a goose had walked over my grave.

"A covenant", said Suzy, shrugging. "That's what my religion teacher said. And something about the relationship between God and his people or Jesus the Bridegroom and the Church the Bride. Only that doesn't make sense to me. How could God marry anybody? Or even Jesus? When anyone says that Jesus got married, the Christians freak out. I think Islam makes more sense. God doesn't need to get married, but people do. And everybody should get married, even imams."

"Should. You make it sound like a duty."

"It is a duty", said Suzy. "Aisha told me—"

But whatever it was that Aisha had told her I was never to discover. There was a clatter of footsteps on the metal staircase, and with one motion, the brother turned out the light. We all sat in the dark, listening, as three or four men outside cracked drunken jokes and guffawed. Someone banged his fist on the door.

"Hallo", said a voice, speaking in a falsetto. "Hallo!"

Someone burst into snorts, and there was more muffled hilarity. My mouth was dry. I clutched my shoulder bag closer to me and felt in my pocket for my lighter.

"*Raus, kleine Mäuschen*", said the same falsetto voice.

The banging resumed. "Ouch", said a lower voice, among snickers. "That hurts."

"So get a bat, you idiot."

"I have one."

"So give it here. Ach! Stand back there."

I took Suzy's hand and bent toward her ear. Her hair tickled my nose, and I resisted the urge to sneeze. "Don't say a word. When I get up, follow me, okay?"

The bat hit the door with a sickening clang. The men outside roared with laughter.

"*Scheisse!* That hurt!"

"Give it here, you pansy. I'll show you how it's done."

The door clanged again. The bat seemed to tumble to the ground, and there were catcalls and cursing.

"Is there really anybody in there?"

"Yes, of course. I saw him run down the stairs."

"Helmut said there were customers inside, too. Women."

There was much joking about this, and I felt sick to my stomach. In Pakistan, I had had the luxury of not understanding what the mob was yelling.

"God, this really does hurt. You try."

"Wimp."

Clang.

"Ach! *Scheisse!*"

Roars of laughter.

"That's a strong door."

"Maybe we should smoke them out."

"Are you crazy? You'll burn down the whole house."

95

"Yeah, why not?"

Suzy's hand was hot and sweaty. I let it go for a moment to slide my bag over my shoulder, and then I picked it up again. I stood slowly, and Suzy stood too. I let go of her hand for a moment and felt for her right. With my right hand, I felt before me, and with my left I led Suzy to the wall behind the couch. I began to feel my way along, inching past the grandmother on her cot. I could hear her breathing rapidly, like a sleeping baby. I found the edge of the passage and turned. The dank smell greeted me like a friendly dog; I stopped myself from running toward it. Someone had taken a crack at the door again. I wondered what would happen if they got through. A lot depended on whether or not the brother and sister were armed.

Inch by inch, I felt my way along the damp passage and then crossed to the other wall to feel my old route along the second chamber. The music had been turned off, and footsteps thudded along the floor in the direction of the stairs. Were they going to rush the door, or were they going to join in the fun of setting a fire? I tried not to think about it. Instead I strained my eyes toward where I had seen daylight. And then I saw it, and I heard Suzy sigh behind me.

The grey light illuminated the wooden staircase, and I let go of Suzy's hand. She followed me to the landing and watched as I wrestled with the rusty bolt. It moved another millimeter, and then it stopped. I cursed under my breath and blew on my aching fingers. Suzy nudged me out of the way and pulled herself. With a crack, the bolt slid back, and the door burst open. The sun momentarily blinded me. Tears of relief sprang to my eyes, and I opened the door wide enough for Suzy to slip through. There was a set of stone stairs leading up to an alley. Suzy ran up them, and I ran after her. She stopped and grabbed my arm. Her pupils were like pinpricks in her hazel eyes.

"Which way?"

"Wait."

I listened for footsteps, for men's voices. It was hard to concentrate on anything over the sound of my heart slamming into my chest. Then I heard a crunch of gravel, stepped backward, and fell down the stairs. I lay at the bottom, too winded to cry.

Suzy shrieked and climbed down after me. "Are you hurt?"

She helped me to my feet. I screamed silently and sat down again. My ankle was either sprained or broken.

"Come on, Cat", said Suzy, stooping over me. "We've got to get out of here."

From the front of the house, a fire alarm began to wail.

* * *

"I can't walk", I said. "You go ahead."

"I'm not leaving you here."

"Go to the end of the row and see if anyone's coming."

Suzy straightened up, and I caught a flash of her ankle as she turned to go up the stairs. I rolled onto my left knee and hoisted myself up onto my left foot. Gravel embedded itself into my hands, but that was nothing to the pain in my right foot. I leaned on the wall and lowered my injured foot to the pavement. Pain raced up my leg and blotted out everything for a moment, even the shrieking fire alarm. I crouched back down and buried my face in my left thigh, waiting for the waves of pain to stop. I didn't care about the neo-Nazis, the immigrants, legal or illegal, or for Suzy's well-being. I rocked back and forth, cursing between gritted teeth. Red spots swam before my eyes; I thought I would faint. I hoped I would faint. Anything to escape the pain.

Perhaps I did faint for a moment, for the next thing I remembered was a sort of mental fog lifting and the impulse to crawl away from the building. I rolled back on my left knee, being careful not to touch my right leg to anything, and slid myself along to the bottom step. There I leaned my arms on the second step and tried to pull myself up with my arms. My bag slid off my shoulder, blocking my way. I took it off and hurled it to the top of the staircase. I pulled myself up and balanced my left knee on the second step. Then I dragged it to the third. My right knee grazed the step, and my injured foot sang out in anger. I waited out the worst waves of pain, and then dragged myself to the fourth step.

"Cat, Cat!"

Suzy was back. She squatted down and offered me her hand. I shook my head and struggled to the top step. Suzy backed away to make room. I sat heavily down.

"It's all men out there", she said. "Skinheads in black shirts. They're just standing around watching, drinking beer."

"All of them?" I said. "No women? What about old men?"

I had pinned my hopes to the elderly men and women of the town. I imagined them in smart, old-fashioned suits, deeply disapproving of

97

such assaults on order and unafraid to shout at skinhead whippersnap-
pers. In Frankfurt, the slightest infraction of the rules in public called
upon the malefactor a hailstorm of beeps and lectures from passersby.

"I didn't see any", said Suzy. "And there's no fire truck yet."

"You'll have to make a run for it. And call 110 on your mobile. Tell
the operator the name of the village and then say, *Ich brauche Hilfe.
Meine Freundin ist verletzt.* Then find a woman. An old woman with a
shopping bag. Tell her the same thing. *Ich brauche Hilfe. Meine Freundin
ist verletzt.* Got it?"

"I can't leave you here. What if they find you?"

"Better me than you. Now bugger off."

Suzy hesitated. "I can't. You could be raped."

"Again, better me than you. Bugger off."

"No", said Suzy.

"Jesus have mercy", I said. "Give me my bag."

Suzy gave me my bag, and I pulled out my mobile with shaking
hands. I called 110.

A woman's voice answered. *"Politzeinotruf. Guten Tag."*

There were three shots fired inside the house. Suzy shrieked. I
dropped the mobile. The sound of men shouting cut through the wail
of the alarm.

"Give me the mobile. Quick!"

The dispatcher's voice squawked tinnily. *"Polizeinotruf. Guten Tag.
Hallo?"*

Suzy gave me the phone, and I gabbled a description of the situation into it. The operator told me to slow down, she couldn't understand me. There was another gunshot, and Suzy shrieked again.

"Did you hear that?" I said, and repeated the name of the village.
"Nazis are attacking a house of foreigners. There are children inside.
The house has been set on fire. Send help at once."

"Where are you exactly? I cannot locate this call."

"I am on a mobile behind the house. The place is lousy with Nazis."

"Get away from the building", said the operator.

"That's easy for you to say", I said. "I've hurt my foot."

"Stay on the line", said the operator. "But get away from the house."
"Scheisse!"

"What is she saying?" moaned Suzy.

"She says we have to get away from the house."

"Well, duh", said the girl, rolling her eyes. "Come on."

"You go. Do as I said. Find an old lady."

"No", said Suzy. She was white as paper, but she held her ground. "I'm not going unless you go too."

There was no help for it.

"I can't walk and talk", I told the operator. "I have to hang up."

I put the phone in my bag, slid the strap to my shoulder, and struggled up onto my left foot. Suzy put my right arm around her shoulders.

"Let's go", she said.

The pain screamed out like the fire alarm, and I cursed and wept as I hopped along beside Suzy, trying to keep my right knee raised. I sank against the wall when we got to the end of the row and slid to the pavement. The road, which sloped upward to the right, was deserted. The afternoon sun beat down upon the village. The air was acrid with smoke.

"No farther", I said. "We'll be safe here."

"Keep going", said Suzy. "Come on, Catriona."

"No", I said. "It hurts too much, and I don't want to."

"Where are the fire trucks?" she hissed. "Where are the police?"

"They'll be along any minute. The whole village can't be Nazi."

"How do you know?"

"The NPD never gets more than twenty-six percent of the vote in any village."

"Geez, Cat. Do you think those guys out there vote?"

"Why don't you ask them?"

My leg throbbed, and I curled the rest of my body into a ball.

"This sucks", said Suzy. "I'm going to try the next block. Maybe people will come when they see the smoke."

"Good idea", I said through my knee. "But don't trust anyone under sixty."

Suzy hesitated. "But what will you do if—"

"I'll concoct a fine Nazi pedigree for myself. I'll trot out all Dennis' glorious ancestors and claim them as my own. I'll say the foreigners took me as a hostage, and I escaped."

"Oh, *shit*", said Suzy. "Why don't they come?" Her voice raised to a nearly hysterical pitch on the last syllable.

"If you're going, go", I said. "I wish to God I had a drink."

Suzy ran. I turned my head to see her fly across the street, her orange hair whipping around her head. No one appeared to chase after her. I sank back into my knee. The alarm stopped ringing, and in the sudden silence, I thought I could hear children crying. But then the quality of the sound changed, and I thought it must be a woman, or even a man. I wondered dully if any of the bullets had hit their human targets, and if anyone had been killed. Perhaps news vans would turn up before the firefighters did. One more attack on foreigners by neo-Nazis. The *Wessis* would click their tongues. The mysterious émigrés would be photographed climbing into a police van. The *Ossis* would raise their eyebrows. Beside the big stories on the attack, there would be little columns on the smuggling of illegal immigrants. But then I realised that the Dresden bombing would drive all this to the back pages anyway.

I had forgotten. Poor Dresden, once again bombed by foreigners. And now these innocent foreigners—and I, for I didn't consider myself innocent—were being punished for it. I prayed that the others were alright—the old lady with her worry beads, the old man with my cigarettes, the mother, the teenager kicking at the gravel, the three children, the smuggler, his sister, and all the stupid Nazis who had had the bright idea of smashing the restaurant in the first place.

I looked up over my knee, or thought I did. Dennis was sitting against the opposite wall, listening to his MP3 player through headphones. His clear blue eyes, so startling against his black eyelashes, looked dreamily over my head.

"Deniz", I said.

He looked down and his eyes caught mine. He smiled.

"I'm sorry", I said.

He took his earphones off and inclined his head.

"I'm sorry", I said again.

Dennis shrugged. "*Tja*", he said. "We bombed Coventry."

Then I passed out, if I had not passed out already, and I remember nothing after that until a shadow fell over my face, and then a bright light.

"Cat", said Suzy. "Cat, the police are here."

I remember looking into the face of the policewoman; she had green eyes, too. For a moment, I thought she was my cousin Kristen and wondered what she was doing there. I don't remember what happened next, but Suzy told Dennis at the hospital that when the policewoman asked me my name, I had said, "Katarina Erlichmann", before I passed out again. Suzy spread the story around as a tribute to my complete devotion to my fiancé. Later she must have regretted that; it must have made her friends sniff when Dennis left me.

I wish I believed in the motive she attributed to my subconscious. It is much more likely that I spoke from self-protection. In my confusion, I thought the cops were Nazis, and in my cowardliness, I did exactly what I told Suzy I would do. I invoked Dennis' Nazi ancestors to save my foreign skin.

Chapter 3

The countryside flashed by as Dennis sped down the fast lane. Trance poured from the car speakers, and I bobbed my head along euphorically. I was as high as a kite on painkillers. I liked this; it made me impervious to Dennis' anger. Having spent a night on a cot in a Chemnitz hospital, Dennis was ready for war. Almost before we reached the Autobahn, he was ranting about my foolhardy excursions into the East.

"You could have been killed", he shouted. "What have I told you about driving across Saxony? *Verdammt!*"

"Deniz", I crooned. "Beautiful Deniz. You are so beautiful. I love you. Turn up the stereo."

"You're stoned", said Dennis, but he turned up the volume. "There were riots all over the East last night. Hamburg, too. Antifa busted up a huge Nazi rally outside Leipzig. God knows what happened in Frankfurt. I called Hannah and told her to stay inside."

"So boring. Outside is where the action is. Let's go to a club tonight."

"You can't dance on a broken leg. I wish I understood what happened to you. Suzy wasn't making any sense."

"Suzy never does. Whoot! Whoot!"

Dennis turned the volume down, and I squealed with dismay.

"Why don't you ever speak to me in English?" he demanded. "It would help me learn more. I understand only half of what English people say, and it makes me feel stupid."

"Beautiful Deniz, if I began speaking to you in English, I would forget how to speak German."

"*Quatsch.*"

"I want to preserve my beautiful Hessian accent. It convinces everyone except Hessians. I tell them I'm from Mainz. Whoot Whoot! Turn up the volume."

"I'm serious", said Dennis. "I want to speak English the way you do."

"No, you don't, my little fuzzy duckling. You should find an English girl with a proper Oxford accent."

"Or Canadian", said Dennis waspishly. "A real Canadian."

I said something unnecessarily rude about real Canadians and reached for the dial. Dennis slapped my hand away. I slapped back.

"Stop it", said Dennis. "I'm doing 180 kilometres an hour, you crazy stoned woman."

"So what?"

"*Schön. Ach!* Stop that. Don't make me tie you down."

"Ooh, baby."

Dennis laughed softly but decided to take a firm line. "Get serious, please. I need you to think for a minute."

I looked out my window and sighed. "So boring."

"My mother says the lawyer needs your birth certificate and your divorce papers at the translator's office."

I felt pain gently wedge its way in past the drugs, and I groaned in frustration.

"What was that?"

"Dennis, I don't want to talk about it. You'll kill my buzz. Please don't kill my buzz. Please. Besides, I don't have my annulment yet."

"That doesn't matter. We can cut our way through the paper jungle first. It's not like in Scotland, you know, where you can just get married. We have to make an appointment with the Rathaus well in advance. And booking a hall is a nightmare."

"No hall", I said. "No hall until after the church. I'm not a communist."

"My mother wants to know how long you think the annulment will take. She's on the verge of calling Uncle Franz to see if he can call the Archbishop of Westminster."

That was it for my buzz.

"No", I said sharply and screamed as my foot hit the floor.

Dennis cursed a blue streak as he checked his blind spot, switched lanes, and pulled over onto the shoulder. Tears of pain dribbled down my face. Dennis got out of the car. I grabbed my bag and with shaking hands felt for my bottle of pills. There was a paper cup of day-old coffee in the cup holder. I washed down three pills with the coffee and leaned back into the seat with my eyes shut. Dennis opened the door and crouched down.

"Don't touch my leg", I said.

"Are you okay?"

"I will be as soon as the drugs kick in."

Dennis got up.

After a long minute, I looked at him staring down the highway. "I'll be okay, Dennis. It's just a simple fracture."

"They said you had a concussion. You blacked out twice."

"Well, I did fall backward down a flight of stairs, so that's no big surprise."

Dennis kicked the gravel, and I remembered the teenage boy in the restaurant cellar. Nobody had told me what had happened to the others, and I was afraid to ask. Dennis suddenly crouched down again.

"Is that what really happened?"

"That's what really happened."

"Suzy said the Nazis never saw you, but—"

"They never did see us. I wouldn't have known who they were if it weren't for the songs."

"*Arschlochen.*"

"How many died in Dresden Bahnhof, Dennis?"

"Five", said Dennis.

"Injured?"

"I don't remember. Fifty-six or something like that."

"It kind of makes you see the assholes' point of view, doesn't it."

"No, it doesn't, Cat. Don't ever say that to anyone else."

"You think 9/11 can't happen to Germany? Or 7/7?"

"Historically speaking, we've had them already", said Dennis. "And it was the fault of people like those Nazis who broke your leg."

"I broke my leg on my own. That reminds me. Suzy blames the Chancellor for the Dresden Bahnhof bombing, by the way."

"That's just her stupid nonsense", said Dennis, frowning. "Whoever set the bomb is to blame."

The drugs were beginning to work. I could feel the pain recede into the distance. On impulse, I reached out and touched my boyfriend's face. He leaned into my hand.

"Thank you", I said.

"What for?"

"For being you. So beautiful. So intelligent. So kind."

I could feel the tears springing to my eyes.

"*Also*", said Dennis. "The drugs are working, aren't they?"

I nodded. I could all but feel the endorphins sliding through my body, touching every part that hurt, erasing every worry or fear.

Dennis got up, pushed back my hair, and kissed me. "Is there anything I can do for you?"

"Yes", I said. I turned my head away and shut my eyes. "You could turn up the CD player."

I was still floating on a smooth sea of drugs and music when Dennis parked a half block from our house. The air was warm, and the scent of the summer roses added another layer of bliss. Marcus was waiting for us by our gate, concern written all over his bespectacled face. He was a lot better-looking than I remembered. By now I was tired of the effort of speaking German and was indulging Dennis' request to speak to him in English. As Dennis made his way around the car, I rolled down the window and crooned, "Mark of the evening, beautiful Mark."

Marcus came over and looked uneasily at Dennis. "Is she all right?"

"She's completely stoned out of her mind."

"This early in the day?"

"Ha, ha, ha", said Dennis. "Shut up. Get the crutches out of the back seat. I'm going to lift her out."

"I love you, Marcus. Do you speak English at all?"

"Not a blessed word", said Marcus in English.

"You're so beautiful. If Dennis weren't so obviously straight, I'd be right jealous."

"Thank you very much, Catriona. That's very kind of you."

"I think you are the only gay guy in Hessen who hasn't hit on Dennis."

"And Rheinland-Pfalz", said Marcus. "Give credit where credit is due."

"Don't encourage her", said Dennis in German. "She's been like this since Eisenach, and it's driving me crazy."

"Well, you always complain that she doesn't express her emotions."

"Shush", said Dennis. "Put your good foot down on the ground, Catriona, and hold on to me. There we are. Give me the crutches, Marcus."

"Expressing emotions is dangerous", I said. "A whole rammie expressed their emotions, and now my leg's in a stookie."

There was a pause, and Marcus raised an eyebrow. "I didn't get that last part. Was that English?"

"Don't ask me", said Dennis wearily. "It might be Scottish."

"Ha, ha, ha", I said. "Just you wait, Henry Higgins. Just you wait."

I hopped along the pavement.

"*Scheisse*", said Dennis. "Slow down."

Michael came looming out of the gate. He was half a head taller than Dennis and broader across the chest by far. Like Marcus, he seemed to have grown much more handsome overnight.

"Michael! I'm so happy to see you!"

Marcus snickered. Dennis punched him in the arm.

"Hallo", said Michael in his deep voice, surprised to hear English.

"Catriona is on painkillers", said Dennis in a dignified tone. "Don't do that, Cat. Michael, would you undo the latch?"

"So it's true then", said Michael, opening the gate. "Suzy told Kurt this insane story about Nazis."

"I hate Suzy, I do", I said.

"Kurt said she saved your life."

"She most certainly did not. But I'll tell you something for free. She fancies Dennis, and I hate anyone who fancies Dennis. Except Marcus."

"I don't fancy Dennis, by the way", said Marcus. "But I am fascinated by these revelations. Dennis says you are never jealous."

"Ha", I said. "I suffer the tortures of the damned."

"*Schön*", said Dennis grimly. "I am calling the doctor. Give me your bag. I want to see your pills."

"Don't take away my pills", I said, clamping my bag between my arm and my crutch. "They're my best pals."

"How are you going to get her upstairs?" asked Marcus.

"I'm going to carry her. Open the door."

"Better let me do it", said Michael.

"No", said Dennis. "I can do it."

"You'll drop her."

"I won't."

I listened to the negotiations with interest. Eventually, Marcus took the crutches, my shoe, and my bag and went inside. Dennis picked me up and followed. Michael walked behind to prevent disaster, he said. It seemed like a parade, and I said so. I nestled my nose into Dennis' neck and breathed in.

"How long has she been like this?" said Michael.

"Hours", said Dennis. "Cat, don't do that, or I'll fall."

"You should let me—"

"No. Just stop a second. I need to shift my balance."

"Personally, I find it a refreshing change", piped up Marcus from the landing. "Whatever she's on, I want some."

"Shut up", said Dennis. "It's not funny. She hit her head, you know. She had a concussion. I'll bet those *Ossi* doctors have no idea how to honk or to trumpet."

"Don't worry", said Michael. "I was like that when I broke my collarbone. Loopy for hours."

"Man, she wasn't playing football. She got caught in a freaking Nazi attack."

"You need to relax", said Michael.

"*Scheisse*", said Dennis. "The post. I forgot the post. Could you get it, please?"

"Don't move", said Michael. He clattered down the steps.

"So beautiful", I said.

"Shh."

Michael came back up the stairs. "You have an electric bill and two letters from England."

"Great", said Dennis. "Thanks."

A troubling thought came buzzing out of the air, but I batted it away. Dennis unlocked the door and, staggering a little, carried me to the bedroom and deposited me on the bed. I thought this was an excellent idea and said so. I wiggled over to make room.

"Ah, not right now", said Dennis. "We have guests."

"So boring."

"Can I get you anything?"

"Music, please."

Dennis dug in his pocket for his MP3 player. I took it and fitted the earphones into my ears. I settled into the pillows and let the music wash into me. My leg was beginning to trouble me again; I sank deeper into the sound to escape. Dennis left the room, but soon came back and touched my shoulder. I sighed and took out an earphone.

"Your letters. May I open them, please? They could be important."

"Whatever", I said. I knew that there was something unpleasant about letters, but I didn't want to remember. I put the earphone back in, but the troubling thought came buzzing back, and I could not entirely escape it, no matter how far under the music and the drugs I sank. I remained there a long time, between oblivion and consciousness, until I became aware of a powerful thirst and the pain in my leg forced me to emerge.

Someone had propped the crutches against the bed. I picked them up and hopped gingerly into the hallway. The day had grown overcast; the hall was dark. In the sitting room, the television news was on. The police had been carrying out raids all over Germany, targeting pro-jihadist mosques. Antifa and the neo-Nazis were still marching and screaming at each other, divided by thin, green lines of riot cops. I looked in the doorway. Dennis was alone amongst several beer bottles and an empty pizza box. He watched the television gloomily, his arms crossed.

"Did you drink all those yourself?"

Dennis looked up. "Catriona. How are you?"

"My leg hurts like hell, and I'm thirsty. What time is it?"

"It's six o'clock. I'll get you some water."

"Thanks."

I carefully lowered myself down on the striped chair; Dennis hastened to help me. Then he went to the kitchen and came back with a bottle of water. The post was lying on the coffee table, the tops of the envelopes carefully sliced.

"Did anything come from Westminster?" I asked and thought of the letter lying in my underwear drawer.

"No", said Dennis. "One was from your agent, and one was from some man. I couldn't read the handwriting."

"Jesus have mercy", I said. "Could you give them to me please? Where are my pills, by the way?"

Dennis cleared his throat. "You can't have any more pills. I called the doctor, and he said you took twice as many as you were supposed to."

"I don't care. My leg really hurts."

"I'm sorry", said Dennis. "The doctor said no. And they are really, really, addictive, he said. It's a nonrenewable prescription."

"Too bad", I said, and I began at once to miss my painkiller paradise.

To get it over with, I took out the letter from my agent. The royalties from my books had gone into my mother's chequing account as directed, et cetera. My British publisher was very interested in knowing when my next spiritual bestseller would be complete, et cetera. There had been several letters of concern from readers at my long silence, et cetera. I slid the letter back into its envelope and picked up the second. The address had been typed. When I saw the handwriting on the notepaper, I felt like I had been slapped.

"Who is it?" asked Dennis.

"Nobody important."

"Is it your ex?"

"One of them. Are you sure I can't have another pill?"

"The doctor said no. And he was angry. He shouted at me."

"What about gin?"

"We don't have any."

"Where did it go? We had half a bottle."

"I poured it down the sink, and don't give me a hard time."

"What am I, an alcoholic? That bottle cost me twenty euros!"

"I'll buy you another one", said Dennis. "But you can't touch alcohol until the pills are out of your system."

"Outrageous!"

I read the letter, all the while snatching at the wisps of kindly fog still left to me.

Dear Catriona,

It seems odd to be writing to you after all these months. Indeed, it has taken me a long time and much prayer to our Lord Jesus Christ to forgive you for your heartless attitude toward our annulment. But I always knew that I should be thankful that you did not carry out your threat of appealing to the Vatican. What changed that stubborn heart of yours, I wonder. I knew it cannot be any concern for my happiness or the happiness of my wife. Yes, she is my wife now, in law and also by the Grace of God, as you never were.

"Is it bad news?"

"My leg hurts like hell. Are you sure I can't have anything? Not even a beer?"

"No, Cat. I'm sorry."

"Well, make me a cup of tea then."

I wonder if that surprises you, who never believed that my love for Joanna would come to fruition. You always misunderstood me, I think, and my friendships with my students. Yes, there was an erotic element to those relationships, but if you had read Plato and Aristotle with any real facility, you would have understood that there is of necessity a bond of Eros between the best of students and the best of teachers. And between my wife and me, there has been the final transformation. It is I who am the student now, and she the teacher. That is what I always wanted; that is what you could never give me. You were simply not the woman I thought you. But I realise that is not your fault.

The last wisps of fog disappeared. There was nothing between me and pain. The only comfort was that Dennis had been unable to decipher the scratches on the paper. I shifted and gasped.
"Are you okay?" called Dennis.
"No, damn it."

Now that I have been released from fear, the fear that you would stand between us and our hopes, I feel that I can be generous in safety. I have learned many lessons in love, and I can now look back on the past with the eyes of love. I can even smile on you, Catriona, so determined to preserve what you called "common sense" and "decorum" (really a form of scrupulosity, as I always told you) as you envied that which you could never know. Are you still as jealous as ever? Forgive me for asking. I am so relieved to be freed from the bonds of jealousy, that I am almost drunk on freedom.

"The kettle is on", said Dennis, coming back in.
"Thank you."

I have heard a rumour that surprised me very much, and I ask your forgiveness again if it is entirely without truth. I bumped into Martina this morning, and she mentioned that you have taken a young German philosophy student under your maternal (?) wing. To confess the truth, I laughed at the irony. But for your sake as well as his, I hope this liaison is of a very casual nature. Unless you are very much changed, you are not a fit companion for a young man who wishes to dedicate his life to Philosophy, nor is he a fit companion for you. My poor Catriona: do you now fancy yourself Diotima? I fear that you will forever condemn yourself to the role of Xanthippe. As a friend and well-wisher, for so you may believe me to be, I pray that you will find whatever happiness of which you are capable.

Sincerely, et cetera . . .

"What does he say?" asked Dennis.

"He says he hates my guts."

"So, it is the first husband. Rip it up."

"No. It will serve as a useful reminder of the death of love."

My leg twinged, and I gasped.

"Is it bad?"

"Bad enough. I don't think I'll have tea after all. Would you help me up? I want to lie down."

"I'll carry you."

"Okay, but don't bump me."

"I won't bump you more than four or five times."

The bedroom windows were open. The air was heavy with scent.

"You lie down, too", I said.

He hesitated. "Ah, that is maybe not such a good idea."

"Why not?"

"Ah, well. You know. You are hurt."

"It cannot hurt me if you lie down."

Dennis stood by the bed, thinking.

"Well, then", he said, "I will unplug the kettle."

He padded out to the kitchen and padded back. I squirmed over to his side of the bed, and he stretched himself out beside me. We lay like that for a while, and the nearness was enough to take off the edge of my ex-husband's letter.

Dennis sighed.

"I think maybe I am a monster", he said.

I turned my head to look at him. He looked back, smiling ruefully.

"Hey", I said. "No pills. No gin. No beer. That leaves me only one option."

"I am not a painkiller", said Dennis. "I am a human being."

"You can be both at once. Kiss me."

*   *   *

RE: News

From: "Catriona McClelland" cmclel@wwcath.org

To: "Davis Suzanne" paxgrl86@yahoo.ca

Dear Suzy,

I hope you are well after our crazy Saxony adventure. It's the kind of thing that doesn't get mentioned in the "Study in

Germany" catalogues. Thanks for lugging me along to the corner like that.

I don't know if Aisha has told you already, but I have good news from a religious point of view. Dennis and I are to be married when/if I get my annulment. We don't exactly know when this will be. As you may have heard, this sometimes takes years. However, you don't have to worry about the corruption of Dennis anymore.

Sincerely,
Catriona

*   *   *

My little book was mentioned in the Reichstag, and my German agent called me in a flurry of excitement. She was stunned into silence when I refused to do interviews. My publisher was appalled and remonstrated with me over the phone, citing the relevant clauses in my contract. So eventually I gave in and was kept busy providing German colleagues with sound bites. This proved to be a blessing in disguise, for it kept the fear of losing Dennis at bay. There was relief from another quarter, too: Dennis told his mother to stop bothering us for wedding plans. He told her that I had had a bad shock from my misadventure from Saxony and was under too much stress already. He may have believed this himself. Frieda, from whom Dennis had learned to despise the *Ossis*, said she understood. She was mollified also by the sight of me on television.

Talking to reporters was frustrating for both them and me, for it was clear that few of them had read my book past page five, and I refused to talk about the growing tension over the Bahnhof bombings. Germans love to complain about Germany, but they always get angry when foreigners make the same complaints. I never do; I have perfected a look that manages to convey both interest for the speaker's point of view and admiration for Germany in general. And in interviews, I had a way of throwing up my hands and saying "I am not a citizen" that amused many people, especially my friends. Someone called me "Citizen *Keine*", and it caught on. My publisher was delighted, and far away in his New York office, my editor was impressed. He wrote suggesting that my move to Rome be delayed until December. But despite this reprieve, I was not very happy. I have never wanted to be a public person, and I found it annoying when students approached me in the street. Had my publisher allowed it, I would have used a penname. But annoyance, too, kept fear at bay.

Miraculously, no one uncovered the story of my adventure in Saxony. I told interviewers solicitous of my leg that I had fallen downstairs. Meanwhile, casual questioning of my colleagues yielded no information about the village. The regional police would not return my calls. Finally, I thought to call Santosh D'Cunha in Berlin. He had heard nothing, but he promised to dig. After some hesitation, I told him my suspicions about Jason, the German American in his youth group. Santosh was dubious.

"We get along great", he said. "What makes you think he's a neo-Nazi?"

I told him what Jason had said and, pulling his card out of my wallet, described the Iron Cross and the telephone number.

"Did you call him?"

"Why would I call him? I don't make friends with the ultra-right."

"I thought you were apolitical."

"That's one reason why I don't make friends with the ultra-right."

"I don't think he's a neo-Nazi", said Santosh. "And that is not the number on my youth group list. Should I call it?"

"Call it if you want to, but I don't want anything to do with it."

"And you call yourself a reporter."

"I'm on the religion beat, Santosh. Get me the number of a German jihadist and I'll call that."

"Get in line", said Santosh.

He called me back a few days later. He asked me about my leg and Dennis, and told me all his family news. Finally, he said, "I would like you to meet someone I spoke to in Frankfurt."

"A priest?"

Santosh was always trying to send me to priests in Frankfurt. His clericalism often clouded his professionalism, and he longed to help out priests' fundraising drives with media attention.

"Not a priest. A woman. She has some information I think you should hear."

"Is it about the Nazi village?"

"It might be related. It isn't very clear. Her name is Ursula, and she has a little restaurant in Alt Sachsenhausen." He named it, and I wrote it down in my notebook.

"Can you give me any idea? I can't drive with this leg. And it is terrible getting down the stairs when Dennis isn't home."

"You'd better talk to her yourself. It seems to be very complicated, and I don't understand it." Then he said, "How much do you know about your friend Suzy Davis?"

"Not a lot. I haven't seen her since she left me with Dennis in the hospital."

"What exactly is it that she does in Germany?"

"She's a language student, but she seems to spend most of her time driving around organising peace groups."

"I saw her on CNN the other day, explaining why Germany should withdraw its troops from Afghanistan."

"I'm sure the Germans would love that. She's been here three months at most."

"She talked about reconciliation with the Islamic community in Germany, and the hopes for German multiculturalism. She blames the bombings on the voicelessness of Islamic German youth. She wants to set up a foundation."

"I'm not sure what that has to do with Afghanistan, do you?"

"She might have found backers for her foundation", said Santosh.

"Islamist ones?"

"I don't know much about it. But go and talk to Ursula in Alt Sachsenhausen."

I left a note for Dennis on the fridge and then took a cab to Alt Sachsenhausen. The tourists, mostly other Europeans, were out in full force, walking slowly along the bridges and cobblestoned streets, sweltering in the heat. The wooden benches outside the painted taverns were jammed with noisy Englishmen. British pop music blared from speakers, and the English shouted over it as they drank their towers of beer. The men were huge and beefy, wearing sleeveless T-shirts or no shirts at all. Their hides were livid with sunburn; it hurt me to look at them. The few women they had brought with them were big, too, and wore football jerseys.

The cab turned down a quieter street, one that presumably catered to German tourists, for it offered secondhand music, comic books, and Native American art for sale. The driver stopped outside an ornate metal door, painted an unprepossessing blue. I got out of the cab and carefully navigated the cobblestones with my crutches. The driver watched me with a fatherly expression and then got out of the cab to open the door of the restaurant.

The restaurant was a typical half-timbered tavern set up for tourists, but there were no tourists present: only middle-aged German men watching a football game on the television behind the bar. The place was illuminated with rather dull, yellow light; the sun that made its way through the lace curtains over the one window was dusty. I sat at a table covered with a flowered plastic cloth and read the dishes featured on the paper placemat. They included all the usual Hessian specialties: the cheeses, the sausages, the eggs in green mayonnaise. It was the sort of food Dennis hated and never ate.

A grandmotherly woman in an apron approached my table. I asked if I might speak to Ursula. Ursula wasn't in, said the waitress, but she would be back soon. She went away without taking an order but returned with a bottle of cider, a glass of ice, and a plate of cheese with onions. I picked at the cheese and tried to interest myself in the match on television. One of the men watching was apparently a master statistician and informed the man beside him of the histories of all the players. The man grunted in reply. A wasp landed on my table and marched toward a sticky patch of dried cider.

The time went by very slowly, and I felt trapped by my broken leg. The waitress came back with a plate of sausages, potatoes, and sauerkraut and waved away my protests. Ursula would be back very soon now, she said. For lack of anything else to do, I ate the sausages. To my surprise, they were very good.

"There's Hencke", said the master statistician at the bar. The sportscaster repeated this information and alluded in solemn tones to some personal trouble in the player's life.

Memory prompted me to look up, and I saw the footballer Dennis had chatted with at the party filling the screen, running onto the field.

"His wife gave him the shove", said the master statistician's friend with gloomy satisfaction.

"These women are crazy", said the man on his other side. "With the money he brings in, why not let him have a little fun?"

"She'll get his money one way or the other. It kills me how many of those guys get married. With all the women they could have? Why?"

"They catch them young. As soon as they turn professional— whoosh! To the Rathaus they go."

The statistician looked nettled. These were not numbers that interested him. I picked at the sauerkraut. The wasp on my table was joined by a friend. They walked around the dried puddle of cider. The stationary fan over my table wasn't cooling the hot air as much as it was just moving it around. I felt sleepy and slightly ill. I stopped picking at the sauerkraut.

At long last, the waitress came by to tell me that Ursula had arrived and would see me in her office. She waited while I gathered up my crutches and my bag and led me out into the kitchen, holding the swing door open for me. I got an impression of silver counters and black ranges before being whisked through another door to a flight of stairs. There was a handrail, but I inwardly groaned. The waitress asked if I could manage, and seeing that I could, left me to it. The stairs led not to an office but to the second floor of the restaurant. When I reached the top of the stairs, I took a long moment to rest.

Sunlight streamed in through three lace-curtained windows. The dining room was completely deserted, save for a thin, grey-haired man reading at a table near the bar. He wore rimless spectacles and looked like a professor on holiday. He seemed entirely absorbed in his newspaper as I hopped along the room in search of an office. But as I passed his table, he stooped and picked up something from the floor.

"Pardon me", he said in barely accented English. "I think you dropped this."

He held out a card between his finger and thumb, and I saw that it was identical to the one the American Jason had given me.

"That's not mine", I said.

"My mistake", said the man. "Won't you sit down?"

"I'm looking for Ursula", I said warily.

"Yes. You may call me that. Won't you sit down?"

"That depends", I said. "Who are you?"

Small grey eyes looked up at me through the rimless frames. "A patriot."

I felt the same shrinking feeling I experienced in the Berlin café with Jason.

"Right", I said. "I'm off."

I began to manœuvre myself around. The grey-haired man called Ursula took something out of a computer bag hanging from his chair.

"Excuse me, Doctor McClelland", he said, and I stopped, arrested by the title. I don't use it, and I hadn't heard it in some time. "May I read you something? I think it will interest you. I'll translate, shall I? 'In no other country in the world is patriotism so immediately suspected of fascism.' "

I turned around.

"So you've read my book past page five", I said.

"It's a very good book. And written in very good German. It interested us very much."

"Am I to understand that 'us' does not mean the ultra-right?"

"We understood you to be apolitical."

"I am apolitical. But I have reasons for not wanting to associate with the ultra-right. Family reasons."

"Curious", said Ursula. "Which family would that be? Please sit down, Doctor McClelland. You look uncomfortable. It is not much cooler up here, though the windows do allow a breeze. The Erlichmanns were, of course, under much scrutiny following the war. Your boyfriend's grandfather, for example. Yes, we know Dennis. You would be surprised at what we know."

"Dennis' grandfather was acquitted", I said. "I'm not going to discuss the Erlichmanns. I'm here to find out about what happened in Saxony three weeks ago—if you know."

The grey-haired man seemed to ignore that. The sun glinted on his glasses.

"Your own people, I think, were involved in the 1939–1945 conflict."

"Yes, of course. For the other side. But it's not something I'm comfortable discussing in—"

"One of your grandfathers was in the Royal Canadian Corps of Signals. The other one, the Scots one, was in RAF, am I correct?"

"I'd bloody well like to know where you came by that information."

"It was not hard to find", said Ursula. "Do you know what he did there?"

"He was a fighter pilot. My dad said he never talked about it."

"Excuse me. Not a fighter pilot."

"Yes, a fighter pilot. He was invalided out in 1944. Now if we could return to current events."

"Dresden", said Ursula.

My heart jolted. "What?"

"The Bahnhof bombing", he said, smiling thinly. "You wish to talk about current events."

"Yes", I said, getting my face back under control. "I wish to find out what happened to a family of Muslims hiding in a cellar during an ultra-right attack that afternoon."

Ursula took a piece of paper from my book. "According to the regional police report, there were only three people hiding in the cellar, Raifa Buric and her, er, 'parents' Mehmet and Aida Buric. The restaurant is owned by Raifa Buric."

"I see. And the neo-Nazis?"

Ursula paused and a flicker of amusement crossed his otherwise impassive face. "You are interested?"

"I heard gunshots."

"The police report doesn't mention gunshots. But a man was admitted to a hospital in Chemnitz with a bullet wound in his thigh that night. His companion said it was an accident; the gun went off while he was cleaning it. It was unregistered."

"Will he be okay?"

"He'll ache for as long as you do, but he'll recover."

"Good."

Ursula gazed at me thoughtfully. "You don't believe in revenge then?"

"No. I believe in justice."

"It's more difficult to obtain."

"Apparently."

Ursula took a photograph from my book, and I fleetingly wondered what else the familiar pages contained. Maps? Microdots? Troop lists from 1945? But then he placed the photograph on the table, and my attention was riveted.

"Do you recognise that woman?"

It was Suzy with a piece of white gauze wrapped around her dark hair. She was at some outdoor event, chatting with a handsome, hawkish man. He looked familiar, too. My mind went chasing through the thickets of my memory for the right information.

"I might. Why?"

"Her name is Suzanne Davis. She's a Canadian student here in Frankfurt. She's a friend of yours."

"I wouldn't say a friend", I said. "We're friendly."

"Did you meet her in Canada? You often spend holidays there, of course."

"As a matter of fact, I didn't. I met her here in Frankfurt. In a club. In the toilet. She needed help, and I spoke English."

"Yes?"

I lifted my hands as if warding off blame. "That's all. She thought it funny that I was a Canadian with a Scots accent."

"It's not much to base a friendship on."

"Suzy is like that. And I don't think she knows another Canadian woman here. Her German is very poor, and she gets homesick."

"Do you recognise the man in the picture?"

As he asked, my mind pounced on the memory.

"Yes", I said. "That's Ahmed al-Ahmain. He's a local party boy. A bit of a cokehead, but he knows a lot of important people through his dad." It struck me suddenly that Suzy's hair was unusually natural-looking. I looked more closely and asked, "Is that a recent picture?"

"Yes", said Ursula. He placed the photo back in my book. "It was taken a month ago in Pakistan."

"Pakistan?"

He said nothing in reply. He gazed at me for a moment and said, "I wonder, Doctor McClelland, if you could help us."

"I don't know. I still don't know who 'us' is."

"We work for Germany, of course."

"Are you BfV?"

"We certainly work to protect the security of Germany."

"That's no answer."

"Let us say, then, that we supplement the BfV."

"I don't know what help I can be to you", I said. "I'm not involved in Suzy's peace group, and I don't want to be. I think her ideas are naïve, and I think she's an idiot for commenting on a culture she can't begin to understand."

"We will let you know", said Ursula. "For the time being, all we want to know is if you have ever seen Suzy and Ahmed al-Ahmain together."

"Yes, I have. That is, I know that they were at the same party. I was there too. In the River Tower."

"When was this?"

"In May. Gustav Hitzlsperger—the designer—was having a party, and Suzy got swept along by a German *Vogue* writer. She was being interviewed about Peace Now."

"Did you see al-Ahmain there yourself?"

I thought back to the party, the bare-chested girls, the footballer, Florian and Anna Maria squashed up against the refrigerator.

"Briefly. We didn't talk."

"He's not a friend of yours?"

"None of that set is a friend of mine", I said. "But a few of the women took a shine to my boyfriend, and I knew Florian von Brandenburg zu Hessich at Cambridge."

"That is what we wanted to know. Thank you."

"Is Suzy in some kind of trouble?"

"Yes", said Ursula. "But we are not yet sure to what extent."

"Should I talk to her? Tell her to go home?"

"That would be kind", said the grey-haired man. "That may be for the best. As you say, Doctor McClelland, she is dealing with a culture she can't begin to understand."

* * *

I knew I was for it when I got home and saw my underwear scattered all over the bed. Dennis was sitting cross-legged in the middle of it with a sheaf of paper and an English-German dictionary. He looked up, and I saw that he had been crying.

"How could you do this to me?" he shouted.

"What were you doing in my underwear drawer?"

"After two years together, you think I don't know where you hide things?"

"How did you know there was anything to hide?"

He ignored my question and folded up the papers. He shook them at me. "When did you get this?"

"Yesterday. I meant it to be a—"

"You're lying", shouted Dennis. "Tell me the truth. When did this arrive?"

I sagged on my crutches. "Six weeks ago. Maybe seven."

"Just great. And when were you planning on telling me?"

"Dennis—"

"My parents have been going at my nerves for weeks. I have done all the civil paperwork myself, since you didn't seem interested, and now I know why. And Uncle Franz knows we're living together, and he heated up a hell for me, by the way. He says he won't marry us unless I promise to move out first, and now this. You lied to me, Catriona."

"Dennis, I meant it for the—"

"No", said Dennis, getting off the bed. He shoved the papers into his pocket and strode to the doorway. He scowled down at me. "Don't use that tone with me. I hate it, your I-know-better-because-I'm-older voice, and if you tell me one more time I'm too young to get married, I will take those crutches and break them over your head."

"Be my guest."

"But you know what? I don't think this is because I'm younger. I think it's because you don't want to be stuck with me when I'm older."

"Dennis—"

"I know you only want me for my looks, Madame Famous Journalist. You don't have any interest in my mind at all, do you? Whenever I have an idea, you only listen to humour me. But I know you're not really listening; I see you smiling, and I know you're thinking of something else. And when I get old, you won't have any use for me. You'll throw me out like yesterday's newspaper, like your husband did to you!"

"That's not true."

"Look, I know I'm only an undergraduate, but I'm not stupid, you know. I won the Alfred Delp medal, for God's sake. Although I suppose that's nothing compared to being on Panorama."

"That's not fair", I said. "You can punish me for lying, but you can't punish me for my success. I'm a writer. I'm a good writer. I refuse to apologise for that."

"I don't want to punish you. I wanted to marry you. But apparently that's not good enough for you, Catriona. You can't commit to anything. You won't commit to life in Germany, Citizen *Keine*, and you won't commit to me."

"What does Germany have to do with this? Dennis—"

"No! Don't touch me. I'm not going to let you control me that way anymore. I'm leaving."

"But you can't leave."

"Just watch me."

I backed into the doorway and blocked it with my crutches.

"Get out of my way."

"No!"

"You might be older, but I'm bigger", said Dennis. "And I'm mad enough to knock you over, so move."

"Dennis—!"

Before I knew what was happening, he had pulled my right crutch away and put his arm around my waist to catch me. I screamed. My left crutch clattered to the ground as Dennis dragged me to the bed.

For one sickening moment, I thought he really was going to hit me, but instead he picked up my crutches and left the room. He slammed the door behind him. I heard the hall door opening and the slithering crash of my crutches falling down the stairs. Then the hall door shut, and Dennis came storming back into the room. He scooped his wallet from the bed.

"You're going to be really sorry", he said.

"Where are you going?"

"Never mind."

And then with another bang he was gone. I heard him clattering down the stairs and then another crash, as he presumably kicked my crutches out of his way. I put a pillow over my head and relieved my feelings in a burst of tears. When it was over, I was dispirited but clearer in mind. There was still no gin in the house; I hadn't had a drop since my spree with the painkillers. I decided to make a cup of tea. I got up and hopped to the kitchen and put on the kettle while holding onto the counter. Then I hopped to a chair and waited.

I was drinking my third cup of tea when the buzzer sounded. My heart leapt; Dennis must have forgotten his key. I hopped to the loudspeaker.

"Dennis?"

"No", said a familiar woman's voice. "It's me, Suzy."

"Suzy, I'm busy. I can't talk."

"I really, really need to talk to you", said Suzy, and from her voice I could hear that she was on the verge of tears. "Please, Cat, I need to see you."

"Jesus have mercy", I said. "Okay. Come up. And bring my crutches with you. They're on the stairs somewhere."

I opened the door and hopped back to my chair at the table and my tea. I heard steps on the staircase, and the hall door shut. Suzy, her dark roots almost black compared to the faded orange of her dye job, appeared in the kitchen doorway. I was happy to see that she had my crutches with her.

"You lied to me", said Suzy.

"Oh no", I said. "Now you. Give me my crutches, please."

"I can't believe it", she said, leaning the crutches against the table. "You're my best friend in Germany, and you lied to me. You totally screwed me over."

"I didn't screw you over", I said. "Arguably, I screwed Dennis over, but not you."

"It's the same thing", said Suzy tearfully. "And you lied to me. When I got your email, I cried. But you know what? I was happy for Dennis 'cause I knew that's what he wanted. And I stayed right away from him. And I trusted you, Cat. I thought of you as an older sister."

"You should never trust a woman where her man is concerned", I said. "Especially not an older woman. We don't play fair, and we'll use any trick in the book."

"Then that's what I'll do too", said Suzy. "I'll tell lies. I'll tell him you told me you're still in love with your ex-husband, or that you went to bed with one of his friends."

"Sure", I said. "Whatever. Tell him I've been having it off with Marcus for weeks. He'll believe that. How do you know I lied, anyway? Have you seen him?"

"I saw him at Aisha's today", she said. "We were having coffee, and he came in with your ex-husband's letter. He was worried about it, and he thought Aisha could read it. He said you mentioned death."

"Jesus have mercy", I said, remembering. "I must have been stoned still."

"If you don't want to marry him, why did you say you would?"

"Isn't it obvious? I want to keep him as my boyfriend."

"By lying to him?"

"If necessary. Whatever it takes, for as long as possible."

"That's not real love", said Suzy.

"Do tell. There's nothing I like better than to be lectured by virgins on love."

Suzy coloured. "That's mean. And, anyway, I'm proud to be a virgin. Virginity is the greatest gift you can give a man."

"I suspect many of them find it overrated when they get it."

"Whatever. Go ahead and laugh. But at least I have something I can offer him, something that you couldn't give him, even if you wanted to."

"Oh piss off, Suzy. You don't have the slightest idea what you're talking about."

"You'd let him ruin himself", said Suzy. "But I won't. I want to protect him."

"Men don't want to be protected, you stupid cow. And I don't want to protect him. I haven't been scaring off the jet set out of the goodness of my heart. I just want him in my bed and at my table, where he belongs."

"He deserves more than that. He deserves a decent life, a real man's life, with a proper house, and a job, and children and self-respect. With someone who appreciates his heritage."

"You don't know a damned thing about his heritage. You don't even speak the language."

"I meant his Turkish heritage", said Suzy.

"That's something you appreciate a hell of a lot more than he does."

"And that's where I can help him. You only care about his body; I care about his *soul*."

"What does that mean? Do you think he's going to burn in hell if he doesn't 'revert' to—? Oh, Suzy, you're crazy. Not even Aisha goes that far."

Suzy made some reply, but I didn't listen, for at that moment the street door opened and shut. I heard Dennis' tread on the stairs, and I was so relieved, I thought my very bones would melt. He looked briefly into the kitchen, and then went straight into the bedroom. He shut the door. I reached for my crutches and hopped up onto my good foot.

"Go home, Suzy", I said. "Go back to your activist friends and your Saudi friends and your multiculturalism. Go and fight the good fight for the disaffected Islamic youth of Germany. Try to stop the Crusaders' war."

And that, of course, is exactly what she did.

PART THREE

Chapter 1

Suzy's death made the evening news. Dennis came in from the study, where he had been writing, and sat down beside me on the couch. The storm had broken that afternoon; rain still pelted against the windows overlooking the daycare's playground. I had left the window open a crack; cold air blew into the warm room. Dennis took my hand.

The editors had done a good job. The story began with a shot of police officers with dogs combing the area around the Deutschherrn Bridge, under which Suzy had been found. Next there was a clip of Suzy lecturing CNN on Germany's presence in Afghanistan. Then there was the kicker—a report on Suzy's ties to extreme leftist and Islamist organisations. The investigation had been turned over to the BfV, the Federal Office for the Protection of the Constitution. A man from the Ministry of the Interior made a statement about foreign students living in Germany. The Canadian Ambassador could not be reached for comment. But for all the excellent coverage, there was a major story yet unmentioned. Perhaps one of my enterprising colleagues would discover it by morning.

Dennis twittered, exclaimed, and fussed.

"Incredible!" he said. "I can't believe it. I had no idea she was in so deep. No idea whatsoever. You don't think—. Hannah. You don't think Hannah knew, do you?"

"I think Aisha had her suspicions. I did."

"Why didn't you tell me?"

"I didn't want to talk about her. And when I realised what she was up to, you were gone."

Dennis was silent.

"I wasn't really gone", he muttered.

"You seemed very gone to me."

Dennis shifted uncomfortably. "I think I should call Hannah. She must be really upset."

I put a hand on his arm. "I wouldn't. I told the police we don't talk to her much. And they may have tapped her phone."

"Why did you say that? Why would they do that?"

"Dennis, don't be foolish. Suzy was at her place all the time. Aisha's a German convert. Her husband's a Turkish immigrant. You think they haven't been noticed?"

"*Scheisse*", said Dennis. He got up and went over to the window. I wondered if there was still a man sitting on the corner, drinking his bottle of beer in the rain. The next news item was about the war in Afghanistan. I clicked off the television and waited for Dennis to turn around.

"Let's go out", he said. "I need to get some air."

"KK's?"

"*Scheisse*, no! Unless—." His voice softened. "—you want to? I could call Marcus and Kurt . . ."

I shook my head. "I'm not in the mood for a party. Let's just go for a walk. Maybe to a café."

He nodded and fetched a jacket. We walked along the wet street toward Friedberger Landstrasse, each with our own umbrella, not talking much. The man with the beer bottle wasn't at the corner, I saw. I waited for Dennis to plug his MP3 player into his ears, but he did not. Instead he kept up his uneasy silence. Occasionally, I could feel him looking at me, but when I looked at him, his glance slid away.

The rain was pelting down with a vengeance, angry at the long tyranny of sunshine. My feet were getting wet. I touched Dennis' arm and stopped outside a café. It was one we knew well; it played our kind of music. He followed me into the mirrored room. The tables were placed close together; most of the seats were taken. We hesitated by the copper-covered bar, and suddenly I saw Herr Krause raise a hand from his table in the furthest corner. He was wearing a trench coat and had folded his newspaper. The glass of beer on his table was almost empty; Krause looked like he was about to leave. I carefully led the way around through the crowded room and gestured at the two empty seats by Krause's table.

"Are these taken?"

"Please sit down", said Krause. "Frau McClelland. Ah, and Herr Erlichmann." He shook hands with Dennis, and we sat. "I did not expect to see you here."

"This is our neighbourhood", I said. "We come here often."

"I find the music a trifle loud", said Krause. "This is not a place for an old guy like me."

"Are you on a case?"

"No", said Krause. He found the idea amusing. "I ducked in here, out of the rain."

"We too", said Dennis.

A tall young man with a big basket of pretzels came into the café and chatted amicably with the girl at the bar. He went around the room with his basket, exchanging pretzels for euros, and their rich yeasty scent filled the room. Whenever I smell a pretzel, even if I am standing in an American shopping mall, I think back to Germany: I see the handsome teenagers with mobiles jammed to their faces; I see rain on the cobblestones outside old taverns; and sometimes I see the wreckage of a bombed railway station.

"We found Suzy Davis' bicycle", said Krause.

I glanced at Dennis. He looked stricken.

"I don't see the waitress", he said. "I'll go to the bar. Do you want a G & T or a beer, Cat?"

"Just a coke, please."

Krause looked after him thoughtfully. "Was he very fond of her, do you think?"

"I don't think so", I said.

"And yet they lived together."

"Incidental. We had had a fight."

"As you said. You were on a break."

"Exactly", I said.

Krause polished off the dregs of his beer. "I don't have the slightest suspicion that Herr Erlichmann had anything to do with Suzanne Davis' death", he said and wiped his mouth with a paper napkin.

"I'm glad you think that way", I said. "I can assure you he didn't."

"He's a very fortunate young man", said Krause. "He could have found himself in a very difficult situation."

"Are you still on the case then? I thought the BfV had taken over."

"They have. But I find it interesting, this matter of the bicycle."

"Was it stolen?"

"No, Frau McClelland. It was at the bottom of the Main."

"I guess you can't find mysterious gravel, then."

"What's that?"

"Mysterious gravel. In the treads."

"Oh", said Krause. "You'd be surprised what we can find. When did you last see that bicycle?"

"I couldn't begin to guess. I've just had a cast taken off my leg. I haven't been able to go out much."

"Miss Davis took it most places with her, did she not?"

"Around town, I guess. She often travelled to other parts of Germany by car."

"Yes, a young lady who concerned herself very much with politics."

"Rather too much, I would have said."

"But you, Frau McClelland, you prefer to be the disinterested observer. Your own politics are a mystery."

"I am a journalist", I said. "I prefer not to have politics. They're irrelevant in a journalist, especially a foreign one."

"You don't like to side one way or the other?"

"It isn't my place to take a side."

Krause looked over at the bar where Dennis was waiting for our drinks. "But if you stay in Germany—"

"I won't be here much longer. My employer is sending me to Rome."

"Soon?"

"No. Not until December."

"I would like to see you again soon", said Krause. "Preferably tomorrow morning. At ten, say. If you will be alone."

"Dennis has a class in the afternoon", I said. "You could come then."

"So things have improved between you two? There is no more break?"

"Yes."

"Strange", said Krause. "You don't strike me as very happy, Frau McClelland."

"I'm not a police officer. Murder still comes as a shock to me."

"So it *was* a shock?"

"Yes and no. I told you she had dodgy friends. Perhaps you think I was one of them. Do you think I was involved?"

"I just want to talk to you. That's all", said Krause.

He got up as Dennis approached with two brimming glasses, one light and one dark. Dennis put the glasses on the table and wiped his right hand on his shirt before shaking the policeman's proffered hand.

"Good night", said Krause. He shot me a glance that I could not interpret, and walked off to the bar, where he presumably paid for his beer.

130

Dennis took Krause's seat and leaned over the table. He picked up my hand and pressed it to his cheek.

"Please", he said. "I don't ever want another week like the last three."

* * *

The week after Dennis found my annulment papers was a devil's purgatory: I suffered tortures daily, waiting to be damned. Every time Dennis walked into a room, I expected him to tell me that he was leaving. When he left for class, I wondered if he would return. When I heard the street door rattle, I wondered if it were him or some friend—Marcus, Michael, or Kurt—sent to get his things. I bit back panicked questions about where he had gone and whom he had seen. He seemed to talk to his sister on the phone a lot, and a few times I thought I overheard him speaking English.

To me, he spoke hardly at all. He rolled out of bed in the morning without a word, spent his three-quarters of an hour in the bathroom, and left whether or not he had classes that day. It was the silent treatment, but the silent treatment with benefits: he still got into my bed at night, and when I, heartsick, climbed in myself, he reached for me. But this was no comfort; I might have been any woman, a one-night stand he had picked up in a club, a drunk who had thrown herself at him at a party. We did not speak afterward. But after four nights of this, I broke down and cried. Dennis got out of bed, put on his clothes, and left the flat. In the morning, I found him in the kitchen, eating muesli, earplugs jammed into his ears. I pulled the right one out.

"If you're trying to make me break up with you, I'm not going to do it", I said.

"Leave me alone", said Dennis. "I need to think."

"You've been thinking for days."

"You lied to me for seven weeks."

"Are we going to go on like this for seven weeks?"

"Probably not", he said, and I felt sick.

"What are you going to do?"

"I don't know", said Dennis. "I have to think."

"Will you go home to your parents?"

"I have to think", he repeated and put his earplug back in.

I went into the study and turned my computer on. There was an email from Santosh, asking me to be outside the Eurotower, by the

Euro statue, around ten thirty that morning. He was writing at the request of Ursula, and asked if I would mind erasing the message once I had read it.

I took the U-Bahn to Willy Brandt Platz and went out into the sun-baked street. The area was only moderately busy; business people walked from building to building with mobiles in one hand and cups of coffee in the other. The Eurotower gleamed in the light, dwarfing the benches and lampposts. The lampposts were plastered with student posters; there would be an anti-war demonstration in the nearby park at noon. As I went around the corner, I could see the police erecting barricades in the street. I stood by the bright blue Euro statue, probably the silliest piece of public art in Frankfurt, and watched them. A monument to Goethe gazed blindly over their heads. I stood there for half an hour, watching the police collect around the park and, inside, students set up an elaborate sound system. By now I was used to standing around on my crutches, but I was beginning to think about finding a place to sit.

"That's a lot of police", a voice said in English. It was Ursula.

"What's going on?" I asked.

"A rally", Ursula said. "Do you see anyone you know?"

"Not from this distance."

"We'll approach when the crowd gets bigger."

The park was jammed with students by noon. Several held posters and banners written over in German and English against the war in Afghanistan, against fascism, against the World Trade Organization. The booming speeches were punctuated by the whistles slung around the necks of the crowd. The speakers promised an even bigger, more important rally to be held in the Zeil in a few weeks' time, bringing together peace activists from all over the world. The crowd cheered.

"Interesting", said Ursula.

I didn't see why, although securing a major shopping street certainly presented an interesting challenge to riot police. The police around the park seemed on edge, and eventually one of them barked orders at us to get away from the Eurotower. We walked away from the great blue E and made our way into the park. This was not an easy task, especially on crutches: the students were well packed in.

"Do you see anyone you know?" asked Ursula again.

I looked at the students as we squeezed past them toward the stage. None of them looked particularly familiar, although none of them seemed particularly strange, either. Their faces were more animated than the faces of adult Germans, and their complexions were clearer than those of British and American students. But other than that, they were unremarkable.

"I don't know many students", I said. "I try to avoid them."

"Keep looking."

I scrutinised the stage, thinking to see one of Suzy's gang: the Canadian Mike or Sean, or the German Julia or Lukas. But the speakers were unfamiliar to me. They stood on stage, backed by singers with guitars. There was a young man with shaggy brown hair, spectacles, and a ripped T-shirt. There was another young man, blond, with numerous facial piercings. He would have been handsome without them. Then there was a woman with dark brown hair, loosely braided. Behind her was a girl with fuzzy blonde dreadlocks. A memory popped into view, and my mind scampered after it.

"I know her", I said. "The girl with the dreadlocks. I've seen her somewhere."

Ursula waited. I thought over the past three months, travelling backward through time and geography. The tavern in Sachsenhausen. Television studios. The village in Saxony. Saint Matilda's in Dresden. The Adlon in West Berlin. The smoke-stained wreckage of the sandwich shop in Lehrter Bahnhof. The squat in East Berlin. The anti-Pope rally in Kreuzberg. The party in the River Tower. Stop. I travelled forward.

"East Berlin", I said. "I saw her in East Berlin. At the Axen squat."

I saw her again in my memory, her dreadlocks secured with red ribbons, her hands around a shoebox of coins and bills.

"Ah", said Ursula. "And do you remember when that was?"

"Yes. It was the night before Lehrter Bahnhof was bombed. The Axen squatters had been at an anti-Pope demonstration outside Saint Michael's. I had interviewed the priest."

"Ah."

Ursula looked at his silver-coloured wristwatch and began to push his way back through the crowd. Hesitating for a moment, I followed after him. His greyness contrasted sharply with the bright young, but they paid him no attention. The police barely glanced at him, although they looked searchingly at me. Ursula did not glance at me, nor did he make any dismissive gesture, so I continued to hop beside him. He strode down Kaiserstrasse toward the great railway station where Dennis worked twice a week. The street was busy with shoppers and students, the tourist shops bright with T-shirts and flags. Ursula climbed the shallow steps of the Hauptbahnhof, and I followed him carefully. At the post office, he turned.

"This is where we must part. But have you yet suggested to Suzy Davis that she leave Germany?"

"No."

"I suggest that you do so as soon as possible."

I took my mobile from my bag, but Ursula lay a warning hand on my shoulder. This was so unexpected, I recoiled.

"It would be better to talk to her in person." He nodded a dismissal and joined a crowd heading for the escalators.

Not knowing what else to do, I joined a queue in a cafeteria. I ordered a veal schnitzel and sat down with it at a plastic table. Then I pulled my mobile from my bag again and text-messaged Kurt. I put the phone by my plate, and eventually there was a message in reply. Kurt was in class. I imagined him, bespectacled and shaggy of blond hair, checking his phone under cover of a binder. Putting down my fork and knife, I typed in a request for Suzy's address. I knew, of course, that she lived in Sachsenhausen, but I did not know exactly where. There was a long pause, and then a single letter: Y.

I began to feel annoyed. I had enough drama in my life already without Dennis' friends adding to it. I wondered how many of them knew of our fight and how much they knew about it. To save time, I typed in abbreviated forms of "interview" and "Peace Now". This seemed to satisfy Kurt, for he replied with Suzy's address on Textorstrasse.

Textorstrasse is a pleasant, old-fashioned street of shops and small flat blocks of some beauty. I found Suzy's postmodern building without any difficulty. As I contemplated the doorbells inside the glassed-in lobby, a woman with two small dogs pulled open the door. She held it for me, and I found the elevator. The walls of the hallway were freshly painted, and the gaily decorated carpet was new. I wondered how much the rent was; the place smelled of money.

Suzy's door was obvious: it bore an embroidered Peace Now badge stuck to it with tape. I knocked and waited. There was no sound. I knocked again. Again, nothing. It seemed odd not to just call or text the girl. I knew very little about the technology through which I made my living. Could someone snatch our conversations from the airwaves? If I called her, would a recording device somewhere pick up my signal? The thought made me nervous. I knocked a third time. Silence.

There was a comfortable chair at the other end of the hallway beside a window. I hopped over to it on my crutches to wait. There was a novel in my bag, packed for such waits. I opened it and read for two hours. Suzy never appeared in the hallway. At last, I put my book back in my bag, struggled to my feet and went back to her door. I gave it a good hammering, just in case she had been inside asleep when I first arrived, and then slipped a note under her door. I took the elevator down to the street and waited for the streetcar to take me to the train station. Without my crutches, I could have just walked, and I felt weary with impatience. I had already made an appointment with my doctor to have my cast removed. Two more weeks of hopping stretched before me. The very thought was tiring.

I got on the streetcar, alighted at the Südbahnhof, crutched past the sandwich shops to the escalator, got on a train, switched trains at Konstablerwache. By the time I arrived home, I was exhausted. I leaned on the buzzer in the hope that Dennis was in the flat and would help me up the stairs. But there was no sound. Sighing, I unlocked the door myself and began my climb. The flat door was locked. I unlocked it and let myself in.

The first sight that met my eyes was an empty shelf against the red wall. A row of Dennis' schoolbooks was gone. I hopped into the bedroom and threw open the doors of the wide wardrobe. His clothes were gone, too. And then the bathroom—no hair dryer, no bottles, no shaving kit. The flat was unusually tidy; Dennis must have cleaned it before he left. The fridge door was empty of messages, but the fridge itself was full of groceries. Dennis had been angry, but not so angry that he wanted me, hobbled by my broken leg, to go hungry for food.

And that was it. The long wait was over. Dennis was gone. I sat down at the kitchen table and hung on to my sense of numbness for as long as I could. But then the pain came creeping into the kitchen, and I bowed my head at its approach.

* * *

I took a cab to Michael's building and pushed the buzzer. Michael's flat was on the ground floor. He came to the street door right away. He did not look surprised to see me. He looked embarrassed.

"Hallo, Catriona."

"Where's Dennis?" I said.

"What? Er—I'm in the middle of packing. Come in."

He held the door open, and I brushed past him into his flat. Kurt and Marcus were sitting on the floor of his sitting room, video consoles in hand, beer bottles littering the coffee table behind them. Kurt didn't take his eyes from the television set. Marcus' eyes slid uneasily to me and back to the screen. He raised a hand in greeting.

Dennis was not with them. Michael's bedroom door was open, and I hopped right in. There was a suitcase yawning open on the bed. The clothes spilling from it did not belong to Dennis, and Dennis was not there either.

"I'm going to Greece tomorrow", said Michael, shutting the flat door. "Sorry about the mess. Would you like a drink?"

"I'd like to know where my boyfriend is", I said.

Michael looked very uncomfortable and slid past me into the kitchen. I followed him.

"Er, Dennis? I don't know exactly. That is to say, I haven't seen him since this afternoon. Why don't you sit down? How is your leg? I thought that cast would be off by now. When I broke my collarbone, it took only six weeks to heal. Of course, I was lucky. Apparently sometimes it can take more than eight—"

"Did you help?"

"What's that?"

"Did you help Dennis move out?"

"Er. Why do you ask?"

"Because he couldn't have carried all his stuff down the stairs by himself, Michael. That's why I ask."

"I really wish you would go into the living room and sit down", said Michael.

"I really wish you would tell me where Dennis is."

"It's complicated."

"I doubt that."

I followed Michael into the sitting room, and he stood uneasily by the couch. Kurt and Marcus stopped playing their video game and watched us warily from the floor. Michael looked from me to his friends and to me again. Michael and Marcus looked frightened, like children who have to answer to their regular teacher for the abuse to which they had subjected a substitute. Kurt lowered like a school bully in the headmaster's study.

"Just tell her, Michael", said Kurt.

"I don't want to tell her. You tell her."

"It's not my job", said Kurt and punched Marcus in the arm.

"I want nothing to do with it", said Marcus. "I told Dennis it was stupid."

"Just so you know," I said, "I am perfectly capable of smashing in the TV with my crutch. And I will do it after a count of five if you don't tell me where Dennis is."

"He's at Suzy's", snapped Kurt. "He's moved in with Suzy."

I felt nausea rise from my stomach to my throat and fought it back down. "That's a lie. He thinks she's crazy."

"That's what you think. Anyway, you're the crazy one."

"Shut up, Kurt", said Marcus.

"No. You know what she did. That was a shitty trick, Cat."

"Mind your own business", boomed Michael.

"This is my business. I've known him since I was a kid, and so have you, Michael. If any woman lied to me like that, I would have been out of there in seconds."

"Shut up, Kurt", said Michael.

"Some friends you are", I said. "Letting Dennis run off with that islamofascist leftist twat."

"Whatever", said Kurt. "You treated him like crap. And Suzy saved your life, you know, so show some respect."

"*Quatsch!* If it weren't for me, she might have had her brains splattered by neo-Nazis. I should have left well enough alone."

The nausea came back, and I felt horribly dizzy.

"Are you okay?" I heard Michael saying. Marcus got up from the floor.

"I'm going to be sick", I said.

The kitchen was closer than the toilet. I reached the sink in time.

*   *   *

I was sick in bed for ten days. Every morning I got out of bed determined to do better, to get on with it, to go to work. But whenever I reached my bedroom door, I would remember the break-up in detail and hop into the bathroom to be sick. After that, I would feel physically better, but I simply could not keep down food. It was if my body, having been rejected, was itself determined to reject. I forced myself to eat simple invalid food—broth, crackers, toast, apple juice—so that at least I would have something to throw up. Morning, noon, and night, the result was the same. I once opened a bottle of beer, and the smell alone made me vomit. I lay weak and shaking on the floor. It occurred to me several times that I might be dying, and I didn't much care. Marcus called my mobile three times a day; eventually, he started turning up at the door.

"Catriona, let me in, please."

"Go away, Marcus. I feel like hell."

"I am worried about you. I'd like to see you."

"I don't want to see anyone. Go away."

But time, as they say, heals all wounds. Eventually, I started to feel better and even bored. Robbed of any other escape, I had taken refuge in sleep. But I couldn't sleep forever, and so I got up and sought distraction through reading. Dennis had once bought a set of Dickens novels and, even though he had soon found them dull, doggedly read his way through them. I nibbled crackers and read *Great Expectations*. Miss Havisham had my complete sympathies, and I thought Pip was a louse. I was at the part where Estella announces her engagement when the buzzer sounded. I had a look at myself in the hallway mirror. I was as pale as a wraith, and my hair was a tri-toned mess. Dark and silver roots spread like night through my caramel-dyed hair. There was no way I would let a man—even a gay man—see me looking like that.

"Go away, Marcus."

"Darling!" said a woman. She spoke English with a thick Italian accent. "It is I, darling, Anna Maria! I have brought Silke with me. We want to see you."

Tears sprang to my eyes. It didn't take much to make me cry, and I suddenly realised I was lonely not just for Dennis but for people in general.

"I look like hell, and the place is a mess."

"That doesn't matter, darling. We will soon make all that better."

I buzzed open the street door, unlocked the flat door, and got back into bed. There was a clicking of stiletto heels on the stairs and a jingle of bracelets as Anna Maria pushed open the door.

"Darling! Where are you?"

Anna Maria looked in the bedroom door. Her shiny curtain of jet black hair hung to her waist, and she was perfectly made up. Behind her was Silke, looking impossibly blonde and arrogant. Anna Maria was carrying a basket of luxury groceries. She dropped it on the floor with a crunch and shrieked. "Darling! You look terrible!"

She flew to the bed and wrapped me in her perfectly toned arms. I breathed in the scent of her own personal Guerlain perfume and felt ready to weep once again.

"It stinks in here", said Silke. "What have you been doing to yourself?"

"Silke, can you not see that she is ill? *Santo cielo*, Catriona. You are all skin and bones, darling."

"You can open the window if you want", I growled, and Silke, trailing cigarette smoke, crossed the room to do so. She then sat herself down on my vanity table and crossed her thin ankles. Her gold strappy sandals were miracles of the craftsman's art.

"We saw Dennis", she said. "He was shopping on the Zeil with Suzy."

"Was she wearing a burka?"

Silke ignored that. "He said that you had broken your engagement. I must say that I was surprised."

"Bollocks. He left me."

"Yes. That's what I thought", said Silke coolly. "Although what he sees in that dumb cow is a mystery to me."

"Well, Silke, you were the one who introduced her to him."

Silke shrugged. "I thought she was a nice little thing, political, idealistic. But now she's just a bore. She's gone all religious, and what is worse, she's got Ahmed all religious, too. He goes out hardly anywhere, and the two of them are always at some lecture, I hear."

"Didn't he get her all religious?" I asked. "When I first met her she was a typical lefty."

"Ahmed has always been completely anti-religion", snapped Silke. "The first thing he does when Ramadan rolls around is to get out of Saudi. No, it's Suzy. She's obsessed."

"Silke is a little bit bitter", said Anna Maria with a touch of malice. "She wanted Ahmed for herself."

Silke shrugged.

"He's good in bed, but—" she shrugged again. "I've had better, and he doesn't really respect women, deep down, you know. He despises us decadent Western women."

"Suzy says the best thing you can give a man is your virginity", I said.

Anna Maria shrieked with laughter, and even Silke smiled.

"I wonder if she still thinks that", she said.

139

I burst into tears and was once again squashed against Anna Maria's perfumed bosom. Silke gazed at our tableau with detachment and got up to throw her cigarette butt out the window.

"The best way to get over a man is to get a new one", she said.

"I don't want a new one."

"That is not the point. The point is to feel better. Come, you look like shit. When was the last time you ate?"

"Every time I eat, I throw up."

"Are you pregnant?"

"Ha, ha, ha. Anyway, if I look like shit, I can't get a new man, can I?"

"But, darling, we are here to fix that", said Anna Maria. "It will be fun."

"You can't fix this cast on my leg."

"No problem", said Silke. "We will cut it off."

"You will not. It isn't supposed to come off for a week."

"I think it is cute", said Anna Maria. "It makes you look fragile, darling. Like a baby bird. We will carry you everywhere in our arms."

The prospect of going out of doors appealed to me. Anna Maria's Cadillac would serve as a protection from the real world while taking me away from my self-imposed prison. I threw off my sweaty sheets.

"Where are we going?" I asked.

"Everywhere", said Anna Maria.

After my long-postponed sponge bath, I allowed them to carry me away. I didn't feel embarrassed; I knew that there was a price tag hanging from their munificence and that eventually I would be presented with a bill. Even before I had finished my bath, Silke was sketching out an interview she wanted to do with me for German *Vogue*, and Anna Maria was telling me about Florian's cultural soiree that evening. She gaily enumerated the amusing guests who would be there, and I realised that my standing among the butterfly set had gone up despite having been abandoned by Dennis. For that, I had my little book to thank.

It was an amusing, butterfly afternoon. The loss of Dennis receded to a dull ache that made its presence known only occasionally. I gave myself up to the ministrations of colourists and beauticians, knowing full well that Florian, via Anna Maria's wallet, was footing the bill. At the salons, Anna Maria and Silke sat in chairs next to me gossiping in English about the latest fashions. I had never heard Anna Maria speak German; I'm not convinced she knew much beyond standard tourist phrases. I immersed myself in their chatter; it seemed wonderful that they could wrest so much enjoyment out of such small details: the cut of a dress, the charm hanging from the strap of a handbag. It would have been nice to have been a woman like those women—if only I had had the money. And it was a great relief to emerge from each salon progressively cleaner, younger, more hairless of limb, and more beautiful of head. I even worried down a salad without ill effect.

"And now," said Anna Maria, "we shop."

There I drew the line. Anna Maria grew agitated, and Silke became gradually more acid and sarcastic, but I refused to allow Anna Maria to buy me a thousand-euro dinner dress, and I refused to buy it myself. Then it struck Anna Maria that she herself had a closetful of dresses, any one of which would suit me very well, were I not so small-breasted. This was a cue to Silke, whom I resembled in build, to contemplate her own wardrobe, and she admitted that she had a few dresses that might be suitable for Florian's dinner party. I was touched, for I could see that loaning me a dress went rather against Silke's conscience. Silke believed life was a competition against all other women: for men, for money, for party invitations. She preferred women less successful than herself and less likely to detract from her golden beauty. If I were a blue-eyed blonde, I don't think Silke would have allowed me into her orbit at all. But as it was, I was a green-eyed brunette, and she did not even flinch when I put on her expensive emerald frock. The neckline slithered past my sternum. Anna Maria taped it in place. She stepped back and clapped her hands.

"You look like sex on legs, darling!"

"Sex on leg", I said sourly, but I was pleased at what I saw in the mirror. I hopped experimentally on my spike-heel shod foot.

"I know a man who would pay hundreds of euros for that", said Silke. "He likes crippled women of all kinds."

I thought of Dennis, who by the standards of this world had got it all for free, and began to feel ill again. There was something untrustworthy about Silke's posh bedroom, the slithery dress, the spike-heeled pumps we all wore. It was a world of gauze and spun sugar, and all too soon it would tear, dropping me back into my smelly, empty bed. After that, the convent loomed with its narrow cell and its boarders' kitchen. I belonged there even less than here.

"Now don't cry, darling", said Anna Maria. "You'll ruin your beautiful face. Silke is only joking, aren't you darling? Bring me a tissue."

"I never joke about such things", said Silke severely. "It is not kind to joke about cripples. It is cruel."

Despite everything, I giggled. Silke had almost no sense of humour whatsoever. The thought cheered me to such an extent I even risked a glass of champagne on our way to dinner. The bubbles fizzled gaily down my throat, and I squeezed Anna Maria's hand fondly as she predicted my numerous sexual conquests, crutches or no crutches.

* * *

Florian had borrowed or rented a yacht for his cultural dinner party, and he had invited fifty guests. We ate at a long, walnut table, twenty-five to a side, as the yacht floated down the Main. There would be a dance later—other guests would be picked up at eleven. Our host's definition of culture was broad—I saw at the end of the table the footballer Rainer Hencke, his hair now grown into a golden scrubbing brush, and there were quite a few models around.

I was placed between an eminent professor of history, apparently an old friend of Florian's father, and the editor of a rather dashing photography journal. The latter was known for his defense of erotica of all kinds, and his small book on the subject was a great critical success. He was said to be handsome, but I found his unnaturally red lips most unattractive. For his part, he was absorbed in the beautiful young woman to his right. They discussed exotic pets. She owned a boa constrictor; he boasted of a komodo dragon in his garden. The old professor to my left eavesdropped on this conversation before shaking his head and digging into the antipasto plate.

"*Quatsch*", he muttered.

"You are not a fan of exotic pets?" I asked. I felt I owed it to Florian to entertain his father's friend as well as I could and threw in a flirtatious gambit. "But perhaps you have other distractions."

"Exotic pets", said the professor with disgust. "Distractions. You and I are serious people, Frau McClelland. Bombs are going off in train stations, the young are attacking each other in the street, and new immigrants are making more and more demands for changes. And yet here we are, Florian's idea of the cultural elite, floating down the Main, discussing snakes and lizards."

It was a very German beginning. Germans complain about Germany as Scots complain about the weather.

I did not take his tone seriously, but I composed my face in a sympathetic scowl. "But what can we do, Herr Professor? We are none of us politicians."

"Ha", he barked. "Do? Something. Anything. The immigrants do not want to assimilate into German society. Well, then. I cannot blame them. What has German society become, after all? The young put off adulthood as long as possible; they do not want responsibilities. They do not want to work. And why should they? It is much more pleasant—and less expensive—to stay in school. They drain our taxes, but then they do not want to pay taxes themselves. They learn English; they go to America, where there are not so many taxes. And the ones who stay behind do not have children; again, too many taxes. Too much work. Too much divorce. There is no sense of commitment. There is no sense of Germany's future—only of a new Europe, whatever that will be. When I speak to my students, they seem actively to dislike Germany. You know this, Frau McClelland. You wrote of this in your book."

I perceived then that he was very serious and that this was not ordinary social complaining. I slipped on my signature role as the sympathetic foreigner.

"Yes, but not everyone is like that. The workers—"

"I agree that the workers are committed. The great majority of Germans are still committed to the future of Germany. They say 'European Union' with their lips, but they still think 'Germany' in their hearts. But I am worried about these 'cultural elites' that Florian is so taken with these days, the 'public intellectuals'. They are the tastemakers. They have the minds of the people. They write the scripts, the news stories, the advertising, the narrative. They don't call themselves Germans. They call themselves Europeans. And their Europe is disconnected from reality. A bomb went off in Dresden Hauptbahnhof seven weeks ago, Frau McClelland. Five people died, and fifty-six were wounded. What did you do that night?"

"I was in hospital, actually. I had broken my leg, as you see."

"My children went to nightclubs. They danced. They sang. I remonstrated with them, and they did not understand why. The bombing had nothing to do with them, they said. But I say it had everything to do with them. Do you not think so?"

"I would not like to say", I said, feeling oppressed by his outrage. "I am not a citizen."

"Ah", said the professor. "So you have said. And it was a very clever tone in which to write your book. The dispassionate observer—the subtle flattery. You know us very well. But sooner or later, Frau McClelland, you will have to take a stand."

"Not I. I will soon be leaving Germany."

"But you are a European. You cannot escape what is now befalling Europe."

"Even so I can", I said. "I have a Canadian passport, and Canada is only a border away from the USA, if need be."

"You do not strike me as the kind of woman who would make a run for it", said the professor. "I saw you once on the Zeil with a young man, a German—"

"That's over. He left me."

"*Also*. I'm sorry."

"That is just how life is now, Herr Professor. He wasn't lacking in commitment—I was. But there can be an excess of commitment as well as a deficiency. Whoever bombed Dresden Hauptbahnhof was very committed."

"'Turning and turning in the widening gyre'", said the professor suddenly in English, startling me. "That is how it goes, does it not? 'Things fall apart; the centre cannot hold.... The best lack all conviction, while the worst are full of passionate intensity.'"

"Who is the best?" I asked. "We here?" I shook my head. "Chesterton said that the worst spiritual illness is thinking that we are all right."

The professor pointed his fork at me.

"This Chesterton was incorrect", he said. "The worst spiritual illness is thinking that we are all wrong."

The main course—venison—was placed before us, and the professor had nothing more to say as he tucked into his dinner. He ate with commitment, as if danger could be kept at bay through caloric intake. I picked at my plate, wondering if my rebellious flesh would accept meat, and was rescued from silence when a French singer across the table leaned forward and asked if I knew of any good trance clubs in town.

Florian's dance was held on deck and before the dessert dishes were taken away, a few of the guests had gone out into the gathering darkness to sway to the music pouring out of the speakers. I saw that I was not the only guest with injuries. The footballer, his blue shirt open at the neck, got up from the table with the help of crutches. His foot was swathed with tensor bandages. He swung himself along to the deck, making straight for the bar.

Anna Maria had sat next to him at dinner. She got up herself and came over to see me. Her eyes were very bright, and I wondered if she had had cocaine for dessert.

"Come with me, darling", she said. "I have something marvellous to tell you."

I got up carefully on my one borrowed shoe and crutched around the table with Anna Maria right behind me, patting her excited hands on my naked back.

"Into the powder room", she said. "In, in, in!"

Once we were in, she threw herself onto a settee and clapped her hands with glee. "Darling, I am so excited for you. Rainer was looking at you all through dinner."

I took a new lipstick out of the evening bag Silke had loaned me and repaired the ravages of dinner.

"Rainer being . . . ?"

"Darling! How can you be so stupid? Rainer Hencke, the footballer. Isn't that wonderful? Artemisia kept trying to get his attention, that little bitch, but he asked me if I knew who you were. And I said that you were the most famous British writer in Germany."

"Anna Maria, I am not actually the most—"

"Details! Details! Who cares? The important thing is that he likes you. And you have so much in common, darling. You hurt your leg. He hurt his leg. You can talk about your injuries together. Go, go, go!"

I put the lipstick back in my borrowed bag. My stomach was feeling queasy already, and it lurched at the thought of having to approach any man, let alone a professional athlete. In my mind, I saw those narrow brown eyes clouding over with boredom and contempt, and I cringed.

"Anna Maria. Get real. He's a footballer. Footballers date models. I'm a hack in a borrowed dress on crutches."

"Darling, don't be stupid! Didn't I say he asked me about you?"

Her perfectly tanned, perfectly manicured hand shot out, and she pulled me down beside her on the settee.

"I know that you loved Dennis", said Anna Maria. "He is a beautiful boy, and it is very sad that he left you. But you must be practical, darling. You must think of the future. I worry about you, darling. It is true what Silke says. You look wonderful, beautiful—especially when you take care, like today—but you are not so young anymore. You do not have a lot of time left to get a good man, darling. And there are not so many of them, you understand? Now this Rainer, he is a footballer in the Bundesliga. He makes hundreds of thousands of euros a year. And his friends do, too. Don't look at me like that, darling. I am talking to you like a mother because I love you. Life is difficult, darling. Life is pain. Life is not so much fun without money. I know. And to have someone like Rainer notice you, that is like winning the national lottery. And he is between relationships, do you understand? Maybe it will last a week—maybe it will last forever. Who knows? But I tell you what, darling. Once you're in that crowd, you're in. And you may never have another chance like this again."

Her pupils loomed largely in her irises, and she fairly shook with excitement. She clutched both my hands in hers, and her words caught my imagination. Vague dreams, scraps of wishful thinking gleaned from women's magazines knitted together and took shape. I shoved the nagging pain that had followed me onboard down into the depths of my mind.

"But I wouldn't even know what to say to him", I said. "I don't know the first thing about football."

"That doesn't matter", shrieked Anna Maria. "That doesn't matter! Go to him, go to him! Now! Now!"

She helped me up and ushered me back into the dining room. It was clear that she would give me no choice in the matter. My heart thudding like the stereo speakers, I hopped carefully through the ship onto the deck in pursuit of Rainer Hencke.

He was sitting on a high stool with his back toward the bar, half-listening to something another young man was saying to him. He caught my eye as I crutched toward them, and I smiled ruefully, feeling deeply embarrassed and, strangely, ashamed. The spotlight set up over the bar shone into my eyes, and I shaded them with my hand as I looked at the footballer. I raised a crutch.

"*Du auch?*" I asked.

"Yeah. Me too. Come and have a drink."

He swung a shoulder between me and the man on his right, and I took the bar stool beside him, feeling breathless. The footballer was uglier than I remembered, but his ugliness, like that of a pug dog, tugged at the heart. He seemed younger, too, despite the lines around his eyes. I thought back to the first party at which I had seen him and wondered if it were true that he had two children. He gestured to the waiter and ordered himself another martini. I asked for a mineral water, and Rainer smiled at me.

"So are you a footballer?" he asked.

I laughed, and inwardly I cringed at the false tinkling sound.

"I got this falling down stairs", I said. "You?"

"A really big guy stepped on my foot. My name's Rainer, by the way."

We shook hands. I said, "I'm Catriona McClelland."

"I know", said Rainer. "You're Citizen *Keine*. I've seen you on TV."

"I've seen you on TV, too", I said.

"Yes, naturally. And so has everybody else here. It is always the same with these society parties; everyone knows me, and I don't know anyone. But when I saw you, I remembered that I had seen you on TV. On talk shows. You sounded really smart."

"Thank you. Do you watch a lot of talk shows?"

Rainer scrunched up his face and poked at a tiny pretzel on the counter. It flashed into my mind that he might be embarrassed, too. Perhaps he was afraid that I'd ask if he had read my book.

"No, not really", he said. "Only when I can't sleep."

Before I could reply, he said hurriedly, "Florian says you went to Cambridge University when he did. In England."

"That's true."

"I never went to university", he said. "I never finished gymnasium even."

"You can finish later, if it's important to you."

"Nah", said Rainer. "I don't really have the brains for that. I guess I'm kind of dumb. But I read books sometimes. Magazines, too. I'm really into culture."

I began to relax. Chatting up a footballer was not as hard as I thought. At best, I had expected a thinly disguised sexual negotiation or a frightening battle of wits.

"What kind of culture?" I asked.

"Art", said Rainer. "I want to learn more about art. And literature. Sometimes I go to galleries, but I don't know what I should buy. I go with Florian sometimes. He knows a lot. He has a master's in art history."

"He was well respected at Cambridge", I said politely.

"He's a great guy", said Rainer. "He told me I should read your book."

"Did you?"

"I'm going to first thing tomorrow", he said, and he smiled bemusedly when I laughed. "Why are you laughing? It's true."

"Okay, okay. I believe you."

"Good", said Rainer. "Anna Maria says you recently broke up with your boyfriend."

My heart jolted, but I smiled and said, "Life goes on."

"Found anyone new yet?"

"No."

"Me neither", said Rainer. "I had a break-up, too."

"That's too bad", I said.

Rainer said, "Not for me", and laughed. Two phantom children came unbidden to my mind, and I shooed them away. I sipped at my mineral water.

"So who's your favourite artist?" I asked.

"Wassily Kandinsky", said Rainer. "I bought one of his paintings already. A little one from a dealer in Bremen. And I have *Komposition VIII* tattooed to my arm."

"Now I know you're joking", I said.

"I'm not", said Rainer. "Want to see?"

"Of course."

He unbuttoned his left cuff and then nonchalantly began to unbutton his shirtfront. His chest was as white, hairless, and well-defined as that of a marble statue. Below his pectorals, his skin stretched tight over abdominal and oblique muscles. Rainer slid his left arm out of its sleeve and presented me with a broad and sinewy shoulder.

"See? Isn't that cool?"

His arm was resplendent with circles, semi-circles, angles, and lines both curved and straight. Red, green, blue, yellow—it was a perfectly reproduced Kandinsky painting in miniature. I couldn't resist; I traced my finger across his bicep.

"It's beautiful", I said, and at that moment my eye fell on the thin gold medallion hanging from a slender chain around his neck.

"Oh dear God."

"What?" said Rainer, looking down.

"What's that?" I said, although I already knew.

"That's the Virgin Mary", said Rainer. "Are you Catholic?"

"Yes."

"My whole family is Catholic. We're Bavarians."

"I see."

"This is the Miraculous Medal. My granny gave it to me. It's supposed to keep me out of trouble."

I forced myself to say, "And does it?"

Rainer grinned and said, "I hope not."

He put his arm back into his sleeve but did not do up his shirt. It stayed open over the network of muscles running up and around his torso like rivers to unknown but fabled destinations. The harbour lights twinkled and shone; the yacht bumped merrily against the pier. A crowd of dinner guests leaned over the larboard to shout at the new guests glittering in their party finery on the dock below.

"We should go somewhere quiet to talk", said Rainer. "Neither of us can do much dancing tonight."

He took a key from his trouser pocket. "Florian says this belongs to a cabin upstairs. Do you want to check it out?"

"Wait", I said. "I just need to speak to Anna Maria for a moment."

I took my bag and crutches from the stool beside me and hobbled across to the crowd. The newcomers were coming aboard in an air-kissing, jostling rush.

"Excuse me", I said. "Pardon me."

Granny's Miraculous Medal kept Rainer out of trouble all right. I crutched to a cab on the quay and carefully put myself in it.

"Bornheim", I said.

Chapter 2

I spent the next day cleaning my flat. My first priority was the laundry, and I found an ingenious system for getting my bedding into the laundry room: I tied it in a bundle and threw it down the staircase. Then I carefully climbed down on my bottom and unlocked the door to the cellar. Repeat. While the laundry was washing, I sat in the bedroom and put all reminders of Dennis into a shoebox. I found his grandfather's watch in my jewellery box. His diary was in the study. His mobile was under the sitting room couch. I put the shoebox on the shelf at the top of the wardrobe and placed a pillow in front of it. I shut the door and told myself that I felt better. When I went out into the kitchen to make a cup of tea, I heard the key in the flat door, and my heart stopped. I went into the hall and watched the door open. It was not Dennis who stood there, but Suzy, her hair newly dyed blue.

She said, "Hi, Cat."

"Hi, Suzy. How did you get in?"

"Dennis gave me the key. He's in class today."

"Have you come for the rest of his stuff?"

"No. Is there more? I found your note under my door, and I thought I'd just come over."

"Why?"

Suzy's eyes slid away, and she blushed slightly. "Marcus says you never answer your phone. What have you been doing lately?"

"Partying. You?"

"Oh, I've been giving speeches. And learning German, of course."

"Still chilling with Ahmed al-Ahmain?"

Suzy laughed nervously and twisted the straps of her bicycle helmet around her hand. She said, "I brought up your mail."

I stretched my hand out for the post. There were two cards, a bill, a statement from my German bank, and a begging letter from the Daughters of Charity. I said, "How's Dennis?"

Suzy's face lit up, and she said, "He's fantastic." Then she looked stricken, as if she had unintentionally broken something.

"Come into the kitchen", I said. "I've put the kettle on."

Suzy sat down at the table, and I sliced open my letters. There was an invitation to Florian's dinner party of the night before and an invitation from my British publisher to a book launch in London. The statement from the bank confirmed that I had closed my joint account and opened a new one. The Daughters of Charity had sent a small gift with their appeal for cash: a tiny aluminium medal slid into my hand. I looked at it and grimaced at the familiar little figure.

"What's that?" asked Suzy.

"A Miraculous Medal of Mary", I said. "So are you and Dennis lovers yet?"

"No", said Suzy and blushed again. "Dennis has been a perfect gentleman. And he's been reading the Koran. It forbids sex outside of marriage, you know."

"Isn't there something in there about raping women as war booty?"

"Of course not", said Suzy. "That's a complete misinterpretation."

"My mistake", I said. "So I guess you're waiting to get married then."

Suzy looked uncomfortable.

I got up, inwardly exulting, and unplugged the kettle. "Tea?"

"No, thanks", said Suzy. "There's been some drama. Aisha is pissed that Dennis and I are living together."

"Really?"

"We kind of had a fight. You know, Cat, I don't think converts here are taught the purest form of Islam. There's not supposed to be any racism, but I think Aisha wants Dennis to marry someone else. Somebody Turkish, maybe. She was really kind of insulting."

"She used to insult the hell out of me, too", I said. "I wouldn't be concerned. But Dennis not making any moves on you—I'd be a lot more worried about that, frankly."

"You don't understand", said Suzy. "It's a religious thing. We are living as brother and sister. Dennis knows engaged Catholics who do that. And he's really interested in Islamic sexual morality now. There's an emphasis on purity for both sexes, you know, not just women. Muslim men believe in modesty, too. You don't see them running around with their shirts off or lying out naked in the parks. And there's a real healthy emphasis on masculinity. God wants men to act like *men*. Dennis is beginning to understand that."

I didn't know whether to take this seriously or not. I thought of Dennis' doomed attempts to placate all the women in his life—Aisha, his mother, me—and I found myself saying, "Don't give him a hard time, Suzy. Don't make him feel like he's not manly enough. He's had a love-hate relationship with his looks all his life."

"Oh, of course, Cat. I know. Totally."

"Looks are deceiving. Dennis is very intelligent, and he can be easily hurt."

"Wow", said Suzy. "You know, Cat, I was terrified coming here. I thought you'd totally kick my ass this time."

"I've had some time to grieve", I said. "And I met a man last night—he made me think about how I've been living my life. Maybe it's a good thing for Dennis that he left me. I'm too apt to do things for the wrong motives. And I never thought that much about Dennis' soul."

"And we can all be friends, right?" said Suzy.

"Sure. Why not? But I don't think I want to see Dennis again for a good long time. It will be hard enough to stay on here until I go to Italy."

"That's cool", said Suzy. "I'll tell him that. He'll totally understand. And I really wish it hadn't been you, Cat. I mean, I've never broken up anyone before, let alone friends."

"It was destined to happen", I said. "Don't worry about it." As I spoke, my mind sat back and was amazed. This was not at all the scene I had imagined. In my daydreams, I had blistered Suzy with insults, called her every obscene name at my disposal, and sent her, blinded with tears, into oncoming traffic. Yes, Suzy was playing some stupid political game and flirting innocently with only God knew what foreign interests, but that didn't mean she wasn't the better person. She might be ripe for cynical adults, but was I not myself one of the cynical adults? The difference between me and, perhaps, Ahmed al-Ahmain, was that I wasn't working for any political interest except my own. Suzy and Dennis both belonged to the easily exploitable young. I was on the side of the exploiters. In my own way, I was another Florian, using other people, people more talented and more attractive than I, for my own trivial ends.

Suzy hugged me at the door, and I patted her back reluctantly. But when I shut the door I remembered why I had gone to Sachsenhausen in the first place. I opened it again and said, "Suzy, don't have so much to do with Ahmed al-Ahmain."

"Ahmed?" She turned on the stairwell to look at me, her dark eyebrows disappearing into her blue fringe.

"You've been noticed together, Suzy. I don't know what Ahmed's deal is, but I think the police are interested. I know there are a lot of good Muslims in Germany—I'm sure most of them are good, just as most Germans are good—unless they are filled with xenophobia, Jew-hatred, and militarism by charismatic leaders. But there are also some bad apples in Germany. Really vicious ones, who blow up innocents on trains."

Suzy's eyebrows now knit together over her pierced nose, and her eyes grew distrustful and angry. "I don't know what you're talking about, Cat. And you shouldn't be so islamophobic."

"That language won't work here anymore", I said. "The Germans have had enough. They're spooked. And the forces that police this country are very efficient. They don't mess around."

"You don't know what you're talking about", said Suzy. "Anyway, I thought you weren't political."

"I'm not", I said. "But if foreigners want to mess around in Germany, I'd rather they not be you. Go home to Canada. Take Dennis there; he loves it. Forget about the war in Afghanistan."

"Well, you're entitled to your opinion, I guess", said Suzy with a shrug. "See you later."

"Right", I said.

* * *

The doctor's office was a symphony in white and grey. The walls and floor were of dove-grey tiles, and light shone in through white fabric panels stretched over tall windows. My silver-haired doctor sat at a grey stone desk in her white lab coat. I sat straight up on the grey examination table and looked at my white leg. It was dry, scaly, and covered with black hair. The cast removal was over and done with; we were now dealing with my stubborn flesh.

"Amenorrhea is not uncommon after a shock", said Doctor Schultz. "Have you continued sexual activity since the accident?"

"No", I said. "That is, not for the last two weeks. Before that, yes."

I had always preferred my doctor's office to the confessional. The confessional box is dark and claustrophobic, secretive and unhygienic, a very odd design for a place of healing. It is much easier to state one's sins nonchalantly in the brightness of a doctor's office. And even the sharpest reproof from Doctor Schultz—about my occasional use of club drugs, for example—hurt less than the gentlest word from a priest.

"And you are not on the Pill, I recall."

"No."

"Unwise."

I raised my hands and let them fall. "We were always careful."

"You *were* careful. Past tense?"

"Dennis moved out two weeks ago."

"I see. More stress then. Any chance of reconciliation?"

Suzy's blushing face came to mind. Dennis, she said, had been a perfect gentleman. Dennis did, of course, have lovely manners, but like his sexual morality, they had never got in the way of something that he truly wanted. In some ways, Dennis' wants were simple. My cynicism was, for once, on the side of hope.

"Some."

"That is good. Sometimes men have a difficult time coping when their partner gets hurt. And you got hurt in a spectacular fashion, did you not? He might be taking some time for reflection. Men do.

"Excuse me. I'm just going to take a blood test. This will sting for a moment." Her white gloved hands gently poked a needle into my arm, and I flinched. "Very good. I will be back in just a moment."

She left the room with her file and a vial of my blood, and I took the opportunity to scratch my leg. I had worn cargo shorts, not remembering that I hadn't waxed my right leg in weeks. Now it served as a hairy warning against lack of foresight. I bent my knee experimentally and ran my hand down the shin. There was no pain, not even when I pushed my foot into the table. Doctor Schultz said that I should begin exercising it immediately. I eased myself down from the table and took an experimental walk across the office. She came back in with her file, and she sat down again. I sat, too, on a dove-and-chrome chair. The doctor opened her file.

"You're slightly anaemic", she said.

"I see."

"And you're pregnant."

The white-and-grey world wobbled and went blank. Then I noticed for the first time that there was a shadow bouncing across the white fabric stretching across the window. Was it a bird or a butterfly? I wasn't sure. My eyes followed it up and across the canvas.

"Catriona", said the doctor sharply, and I looked at her. Her large blue eyes were kind behind her spectacles.

"This time I really need you to think back and try to remember when your last period began. Was it before or after you broke your leg?"

"Before. I think, before."

"So at least eight weeks ago."

"At least eight weeks. Maybe nine."

"And drugs and alcohol since then?"

"Nothing. Almost nothing. Painkillers eight weeks ago for my leg. Some champagne."

"Eight or nine weeks", said Doctor Schultz. "Then your pregnancy is still in the first trimester. This means that under German law you still have options."

"Options?"

The doctor cleared her throat and looked down at the file. "In Germany, of course, we do not advise termination unless the mother's life—"

"Out of the question", I said at once, almost without thinking. "I'm Catholic."

The word was a barrier, warding off monstrous possibilities, saving me from new depths into which I might sink.

"Really?" said the doctor, sitting back. "I did not know that."

"What do you mean?" I said. "I'm sure it's on my file."

"I mean, I did not know you would feel strongly one way or the other", she said mildly. "You pay taxes as a Catholic, yes, but I did not know you had religious scruples."

"Of course I have religious scruples", I shouted. "Yes, I've done club drugs. Yes, I drink too much. Yes, I run with Eurotrash. And yes, I have sex. With one man, incidentally. With whom I have lived for two years. Living with my boyfriend makes me a sinner, but it doesn't make me a *murderer*."

The word hung in the air between us, dividing us, woman against woman, doctor against patient.

"I'm sorry", I muttered. "I do not mean to offend you."

"And I did not mean to offend you", said Doctor Schultz mildly. "It is merely my duty to apprise you of your rights under the law and to direct you to appropriate counselling."

"Counselling", I repeated, and then in English said, "Oh no. My job." Panic washed over me and pushed my thoughts to Rome. So much for my job as the first female chief correspondent from Vatican City. New York would go nuts when I told them the news. I'd have to resign. My cheque for the little book would tide me over only until December. I was done for.

"Well, you cannot be fired for getting pregnant", came the voice of Doctor Schultz. "It is against the law."

"My firm is not European", I said. "And this is going to make my boss very bitter. I was supposed to leave Germany. He's closing the press office."

The doctor said, "Then you will have to make a decision soon. You may want to talk to the father. Is Dennis the father?"

"Yes, of course. Heavens. Dennis—a father. He's a child himself."

The doctor's silver spectacles caught the light.

"I would not have said that", she said. "He is twenty-two, after all, and did his military service. He is at university? Employed?"

"Both", I said. "Both."

"Then perhaps you should not think of him as a child", she said. "It's not fair to him, and it's not fair to you. You are not his mother, after all."

"No, but—"

I fell silent.

"Yes?"

I remembered myself, exasperated, trying to shock sense into Suzy: *Men don't want to be protected, you stupid cow.* But that is what I had tried to do. And Dennis, furious, yelling: *What do you think I am, some kind of toy? A child? A prize dog?* Who had kept him a child, if not me?

And when I get old, you won't have any use for me. You'll throw me out like yesterday's newspaper, like your husband did to you!—That's not true.

I looked at the doctor.

"No, I'm not his mother", I said. "And I know he would want this baby."

"And you? Do you want this baby?"

"Yes. It is his—and mine, I suppose. Ours."

"And your job?"

"I'll have to talk to Dennis", I said, and smiled wryly. "It would be a new sensation, having to depend on a man for cash. Perhaps I'll enjoy the novelty."

Doctor Schultz pulled a pad on the desk and began to write on it. "For now, I am prescribing you folic acid and a multivitamin. I hope

I don't need to tell you that drugs and alcohol are now absolutely forbidden."

I limped out of the office on one crutch, clutching my piece of paper. The chemist was on the ground floor of the clinic. There were no razors there for my hairy leg: in Germany, pharmacy is serious business. Such frivolities as razors are left to nonprescription *Drogeries.*

I handed over my prescription and wondered if I might find Dennis at Suzy's flat. Calling him was out of the question, of course, as I still had his mobile. But then I remembered. This was one of his work-days. I checked my watch. It was one thirty. He'd be in the bookstore at the Hauptbahnhof by now.

I took the bag of pills with thanks and limped out into the bright sunshine toward the nearest U-Bahn station. Two Canadian girls, their knapsacks emblazoned with red-and-white flags, changed trains with me at Konstablerwache. They looked very young to be travelling around alone; I thought immediately of Suzy and wondered if they were stu-dents or tourists. I hoped they were tourists; I'd had enough of Cana-dian students. They had matching hair: unnaturally straight, with thick blonde streaks. Together they stared at the rail map while gulping bot-tled water. The polish on their sandaled feet was chipped.

"Mike said to get off at Hauptbahnhof, right?"

"No! He totally said we shouldn't get off at Hauptbahnhof. He said Willy Brandt Platz."

"Isn't Hauptbahnhof closer?"

"I don't know. He just said not to get off there."

"That's retarded. It's too hot for walking. My feet are killing me."

"Yeah, but we'd better do what he says. I hate getting lost."

At Willy Brandt Platz, the girls got up in a great excitement and rushed out, giggling, with their Canadian knapsacks. *Don't blame us,* the knapsacks seemed to say. *We're not responsible for the state the world is in. We're Canadian, after all. We're not Americans. We're not even British anymore. Our hands are clean. We're the nice people.* I wondered idly where the girls were going, and how nice they would be to the people they found there. Hopefully they would not have enough time to be overly nice to German boys with girlfriends.

I got off at the Hauptbahnhof and headed upstairs, my heart begin-ning to keep time with the chug-chug of the escalators. The mezza-nine level, bright with sandwich shops and fruit stands, was busy with the after-lunch traffic. I wondered if Dennis' shop would be busy, but before I could find out, the station blew apart.

An invisible hand pushed me into a fruit stand. I fell into blackberries; they oozed purple-red juice all around me. There seemed to be water in my ears; I shook my head. I hadn't gone completely deaf: I could hear an alarm ringing a long way off. My crutch was propped up against a pile of melons. I picked it up and limped upstairs.

At the top of the still-chugging escalator, I could see a million diamonds spilling across the vast hallway, sparkling in the sun. Bodies lay red and ragged underneath them. Black smoke was pouring out from a row of shops, and I saw that the cafeteria was on fire. The bookshop was entirely obscured by smoke. My heart shuddered and cracked.

Dennis.

The hall was suddenly dotted with black and yellow men with white helmets, and as I slid on the glass toward the shop, one grabbed me by the arm. I dropped my crutch and struggled to break free.

"Let me go", I shouted. "My boyfriend works in the bookshop."

"Get out!" shouted the man. He turned me right around and pointed at an exit. I stumbled bewilderedly in its direction, and then I turned back and made a dash for the store. Another man in black and yellow ran to block me, and we collided like two footballers after a ball. "*Journalistin*", I shouted, reaching into my purse for my ID. "*Ich bin Journalistin.* Let me through."

The firefighter shook his head and said something I couldn't hear.

"The bookshop", I said. "Is it on fire? What has happened to the bookshop?"

He said, "Get out. It is very dangerous in here. Go at once to the emergency team outside."

"But I'm the Press. I'm the Press!"

"Take hold of this one", shouted the firefighter to someone behind me, and I felt myself being hurried to the exit by two large men who shouted encouragement while I pleaded with them to let me go. We burst onto the sunlit street into a cacophony of sirens.

"There is an ambulance straight ahead", said someone. "Walk directly ahead."

"No."

I was about to turn back to the station when I saw Suzy. Her face was white beneath her blue hair. Her mouth opened, and although I couldn't hear her, I knew she was calling my name. I stumbled toward her.

"Suzy", I said. "We have got to get in there. Dennis is in the shop."
She grabbed my hands. "No, Catriona."

"He is, he is! It's Wednesday. Don't you understand? Wednesday!"

"He's not there, Cat. He's at home."

For a moment, I thought she meant my flat in Bornheim, and I stared at her. "Home?"

"He's in Sachsenhausen. I got him to switch shifts."

"Got him to switch shifts?"

"I told him I needed him at the rally this afternoon. He's home. He's safe."

"The rally? But then what are you doing here?"

Suzy looked like she might be sick. "I'm not supposed to be here. I mean, I'm not supposed to be here when—. Oh, it's awful. There's blood coming out the door."

"What do you *mean* you're not supposed to be here?"

"I'm just not, okay? Somebody totally messed up", said Suzy and then suddenly gave a scream, "Oh no, Cat! What's that on your hands?"

I looked at her staring at my bramble-stained hands, and I remembered her in the seminary parking lot in Dresden, convincing me not to take the train.

"Who messed up?" I demanded. "What are you talking about? Did you know about this?"

All around us police officers jostled to keep civilians from running into the station. They looked uneasily behind them as emergency workers with stretchers shouted to be let through. Sirens howled through the streets over the shouts and the crying of the survivors. There was a woman with her torso wrapped in a towel as a firefighter led her out of the station; blood trickled from her head. There was a man with a white hood, holes cut for eyes and mouth, who stumbled against me, apologising formally, as he was led to an ambulance. The door opened, and a firefighter came out with a limp white bundle, a child's knapsack hanging from his wrist.

"It wasn't supposed to be like this", said Suzy. "Are you bleeding? Are you hurt? Why is it so dark?"

"I have blue blood", I said. "Didn't you know?"

I wiped my hands on Suzy's face.

She dazedly touched her cheek. "I'll have to wash up before the rally", she said, and I wondered if she were stoned.

"Don't worry", I said. "It's not blood. You wouldn't want to shed the blood of a friend, would you, Suzy? Hundreds of European strangers, no problem. But not a friend. It wouldn't be very nice, would it? It wouldn't be very nice to hurt a friend. Why couldn't you have picked a time when there weren't so many children around? School lets out at one o'clock here, or didn't you know even that?"

"It was early", said Suzy mechanically. "It wasn't supposed to go off until four. Not until the rally—"

"Not until the rally started. And that's where all the police are, aren't they? Is that the idea? Distract them, give them a good work-out, and then kill a bunch of civilians?"

Suzy's white face turned red, and she straightened up like an indignant hen.

"Civilians? The West doesn't believe in civilians anymore", said Suzy in an angry undertone. "I know you're apolitical, but it's so obvious, Cat. Look at Iraq. Look at Afghanistan. Palestine. Chechnya. Muslim children, Muslim women, Muslim civilians die horribly every day, okay? These people, these Europeans, voted for the criminal government that sent troops to Afghanistan. Their Chancellor supports the fascist state of Israel. Why should these people be immune? It's time *they* learned what it's like to be bombed. It's time *they* learned what it's like to see their children dead before them."

Angry tears began to trickle down her face.

"Suzy", I said. "This is freaking *Frankfurt.*"

"Oh, so it gets a free pass because it's in Europe?" sobbed Suzy. "Sorry, Cat. I don't think so."

"That's not what I meant", I said. "Jesus have mercy. Didn't you study history in high school? Don't you know what happened here? And in Dresden? And in Berlin?"

And Suzy said, "What is wrong with you that you do not fight in the cause of Allah, and for those weak, ill, cheated, and oppressed among men, women and children, whose cry is, 'Our Lord, rescue us from this town whose people are oppressors, and raise for us one among you one who will protect, and raise from you one who will help.' "

"This is your idea of helping? And there are thousands of Muslims in Frankfurt; there may be some dead inside."

"God will be merciful to them", said Suzy, wiping her eyes. "They died in the right cause."

160

There didn't seem to be anything to say to that. I left Suzy there blubbing across the street from the station and walked to the taxi stand. The taxi drivers were milling around, talking, or shouting into their mobiles. I found one who was merely leaning against his cab, smoking, and I got into his cab. He opened the door and looked in.

"I think maybe you should be in an ambulance", he said.

"I don't need an ambulance", I said. "Take me to Alt Sachsenhausen."

PART FOUR

Chapter 1

Herr Krause arrived shortly after two, carrying the *Frankfurter Allgemeine*. Despite his stolid expression, there was a holiday air about him, perhaps because of his casual cotton clothing. The August heat had returned. The climb up the stairs had left the detective red and perspiring.

"May I offer you a beer, Herr Krause?"

"Thank you. That would be very good."

I showed him into the sitting room and went into the kitchen. When I returned, he folded up his newspaper and stood. Suzy's picture, grey and grainy, was on the front page. I handed Krause a glass of beer and sat in Dennis' chair. The detective sat back down on the couch.

"Thank you", he said. "You aren't having one?"

"No beer for me. Doctor's orders."

"I hope you are not ill."

"Women's trouble, nothing serious."

"Well, here is to your health. Have you seen this?" Krause picked up the paper.

"I read about it on the Internet. A friend of mine broke the story. Petra Schattschneider."

Krause said, "You told me, I think, that the parents of Suzy Davis were civil servants."

"That's what she told me."

"Your friend Suzy has become a political hot iron", said Krause. "I don't envy the BfV their job now."

"I liked the *Bild* headline better", I said. "*Meine Tochter War Keine Terroristin*".

"She didn't look like one, did she? The blue hair, the stud in her nose ... And yet it turns out she had some very bad friends. Do you have any idea of how deeply she was involved?"

"None", I said. "I knew she was interested in Islamic spirituality, but I had no idea she was any kind of extremist. Perhaps this was stupid of me: Suzy was extreme in so many ways. And I rarely listened to anything she said about politics. I don't have much time for those who get involved in the politics of other countries."

"You yourself prefer to stay uninvolved."

"I certainly try."

"But perhaps not hard enough."

"I don't know what you mean, Herr Krause."

"Don't you? This is a very nice flat you have", he said abruptly. "The old building ... the trees ... the flowers ... the roses."

"Not so many roses now", I said. "They've mostly blown. I should go out and cut off the dead ones."

"Sad, the death of a rose", said Krause. "And of course Suzy Davis is dead, too. No tidy confession. When I look at the pictures, it seems odd to me that she could be involved in the Hauptbahnhof bombings. And everyone I spoke to kept telling me what a nice girl she was."

"She was a nice girl", I said. "But sometimes even nice people do very bad things."

"Like betray their friends."

"Evidently, Suzy didn't think of German strangers as her friends", I said. "Look, Herr Krause, I wish you would tell me why you wanted this conversation. Do you think I killed Suzy?"

"Certainly not", said Krause. "I am not so stupid. You are not the kind of woman to hold another woman's head under water until she drowns. But I do wonder why you lied to me about not seeing her before dinner."

"What makes you so sure that I did?"

"The bicycle", he said.

"The bicycle? Did it have unique Bornheim gravel in its treads?"

"No", said Krause. "It had a branch of a rosebush caught in its spokes."

There was silence in the room, broken only by the sound of children playing in the daycare centre's garden beneath the windows.

At last I said, "I can't see what that proves. There are rosebushes all over town."

"*Röslein, Röslein, Röslein rot, Röslein auf der Heiden*", quoted Krause. "But those are German roses, Frau McClelland. This stem came from a native British rose, a rare breed, the Glamis Castle. You have one such rosebush beside your building. Quite a thriving one."

"That proves nothing", I said. "There are rose fanciers all over Frankfurt. There's a Glamis Castle behind Dennis' school: they have a wide collection of foreign trees and flowers."

"We have ways of differentiating even between this bush and that", said Krause. "But never mind. As I said, I am off the case. I leave it to the BfV, poor creatures. And someone may have saved Germany a very expensive civil trial."

"Do you really think Suzy would have gone to trial?" I asked.

"That might have depended on Frau Davis herself. If she confessed, yes. If not—well, there her VIP daddy would have been to make things difficult for the prosecution. Justice, perhaps, has been served. But I do not like vigilantism, you understand."

"Vigilantism?"

"This death. It is as if someone knew Suzy might never stand trial. Someone who wanted revenge. Someone who wanted to make her pay."

"It seems more likely that her pals did her in", I said. "Maybe they thought she talked too much. She talked a lot, you know. She hated lying—or she said she did."

"The *Catechism of the Catholic Church*", said Krause suddenly. "Does it have anything to say about vigilantism, I wonder. You permit?" He got up and went over to the bookshelves in the hall. Dennis' books were back where they belonged, and from them Krause plucked a fat green volume. He opened to the back. "Prut! There is nothing about vigilantism in the index. I shall try 'murder'. But no—it directs me to see 'killing'. *Also!* 'Human life is sacred ... no one can under any circumstance claim for himself the right directly to destroy an innocent human being ...' What do you suppose it means by 'innocent', Frau McClelland?"

"You are a philosopher, Herr Krause."

"We are all philosophers in the police. Ah, here is something on legitimate defense. 'Legitimate defense can not only be a right but a grave duty for someone responsible for another's life, the common good of the family or of the state.' But does that apply to a vigilante?"

"The only vigilante I know of is Batman", I said.

"Ah yes, Batman. But he operated under state sanction. That white-haired Commissioner would signal for him. So he was not a vigilante, properly defined. 'Preserving the common good of society requires rendering the aggressor unable to inflict harm. For this reason the traditional teaching of the Church has acknowledged as well-founded the right and duty of legitimate public authority to punish malefactors by means of penalties commensurate with the gravity of the crime, not excluding, in cases of extreme gravity, the death penalty.' Oho! 'For analogous reasons those holding authority have the right to repel by armed force aggressors against the community in their charge.' Legitimate public authority. That would not include vigilantes."

"But a spy. 007. The Bundesnachrichtendienst. The BfV itself perhaps."

"*Quatsch.* We have no James Bonds. There is no 'license to kill' in Germany. No, this was not the work of the BfV. Frau McClelland, are you sure you have nothing more to tell me?"

He gazed at me solemnly but kindly like a priest in a confessional, urging me toward true contrition. I felt like the penitent who nevertheless neglects to mention the worst sin of all, not having the courage to confess it, or lacking true penitence and intention to amend. Reluctance to make such sacrilegious confessions had kept me from the sacraments for two years. So to the policeman I said, "No, I am sorry, Herr Krause, I have nothing more to say."

"Understood", said the Kommissar, and he turned to put the book back on the shelf. "Then I shall go. You won't be hearing from me again. At least not in a professional capacity. There is the matter of the roof."

"The roof?"

"The roof of Saint Bernhard's. It leaks."

"But surely that is the government's responsibility?"

"There are complications", said Krause. "There will be a general meeting of the parish next week."

We exchanged a few desultory comments about the parish council, and Krause took his leave. I went back to the sitting room, pushing the *Catechism* more securely in place as I passed. I sat on the couch and imagined what I would say if I had the courage to confess to a priest. Perhaps it would be easier to confess to a woman, a woman like Doctor Schultz in her big, antiseptic room of filtered sunlight. Doctor-patient confidentiality might be as binding as the secrecy of the confessional. It might have been a relief to say to her, "Doctor Shultz, I lied to the police officer. I did see Suzy Davis that afternoon. My motives were mixed. My heart was impure."

Chapter 2

As the taxi drove over the bridge to Alt Sachsenhausen, I saw several ambulances rushing past us toward the Hauptbahnhof. The cabbie remarked that what had happened was a bad business. I agreed. Neither of us said anything more until the car pulled up in front of the tourist tavern with the blue doors. I paid the fare and hobbled inside. The scene before me was the same as it had been before. The same paper menus lay flat on the wooden tables. The same three men sat on barstools staring at a football game on the television. The same grandmotherly waitress greeted me and offered me an apple cider.

"No, thank you", I said. "I am here to see Ursula. I must see Ursula at once."

The waitress looked at me appraisingly and suggested that I sit down. In answer, I raised my red-stained hands. "Please", I said. "I must see Ursula."

Perhaps she had already heard the news, or perhaps I carried it with me on my clothes, for the waitress nodded toward the kitchen, and I limped into it. The stairs were easier to navigate this time, but the door to the upper room was shut. I knocked. There was no answer, so I tried the handle. The door was locked. I pounded on the wood with my blackberry fists. At last, there was the snap of a lock being released, and Ursula opened the door. It swung outward, almost bumping my nose.

"Ah, the famous Doctor McClelland", said Ursula in English. He was as thin and grey as ever: grey hair, grey suit, grey eyes behind silver-framed rimless spectacles.

"I've just come from the Hauptbahnhof", I said.

"I understand", said Ursula.

"You know what happened?"

"I received a text message. Please come in."

The upper room showed signs of recent use. There were beer glasses, partly full, on a table for six. Tobacco smoke still lingered in the air. In a glass ashtray, a cigarette still smouldered.

"Have I interrupted something?" I asked.

"It matters not", said Ursula politely. "I am always happy to see you." He shut the door behind me and twisted the nub of a lock in the handle.

"It was Suzy", I said. "It was Suzy the whole time."

"Interesting", said Ursula.

"Who does she work for? Al-Qaeda?"

"Maybe in the long run. These Islamist cells ... They pop up here and there, many with an only tenuous connection to the others ..."

"Today's peace rally", I said. "It was supposed to be a diversion. I bet the Kreuzberg anti-Pope rally was, too. It was the night before that bomb went off in Berlin. And in Dresden ... Suzy had some event there a few hours before their Hauptbahnhof blew up. She wouldn't let me take the train home, Ursula. She picked me up from Sankt Matilden as cool as dammit."

"I suggest you stay calm, Doctor McClelland."

"And now Frankfurt. You should have been there, Ursula. Alarms ringing, sirens wailing, people screaming, crying, blood everywhere, bodies thrown about, broken glass, and Suzy in the middle of it all preaching about Germany needing to know what being bombed was like. She's an idiot, Ursula."

"A useful idiot", said Ursula. "A very useful idiot."

He went to the sunny window and looked down into the street. My leg felt tired, so I sat at a table adjacent to the table littered with beer glasses and ashtrays. Ursula's long silence rattled me, and I said, "Well? Why don't you go and arrest her?"

Ursula turned from the window, and I couldn't see his face for the shadow.

"It's not that simple", he said.

"Why not? You're BfV, aren't you?"

"No, Doctor McClelland. As I told you before, we work alongside the BfV."

"Well, call up your pals in the BfV then."

"Once again, it is not so simple. Do you know what Suzy's father does for a living?"

"He's a civil servant", I said, and Ursula permitted himself a wintery smile.

"Yes, of course. I suppose one might call him that. On the table beside you, there is a red folder. Please pick it up and read what you find inside."

I did as he bid, and within seconds forgot that Ursula was there. When at last I looked up, the room seemed to have changed, although I could not pinpoint exactly what about it was different.

"Jesus have mercy", I said. "And she told me her parents were *boring*. I had no idea that's who her father was. No idea at all."

"Indeed", said Ursula. "But now you understand that the usual channels will afford us little satisfaction, if any, in this case."

"She won't be arrested?"

"Oh, she might be arrested. But she might be let go. The anarchist son of a Bundestag minister was let go in the end."

I said, "But you must do something. She's liable to do anything. She or her pals bombed Dresden, for God's sake, and now Frankfurt."

"'Dresden, *for God's sake*, and now Frankfurt'", repeated Ursula. "Your thoughts often run on Dresden, do they not?"

The translucent monster of history seemed to rise up from the floor and ooze from the walls. Ursula leaned over the abandoned table and plucked out the cigarette still burning in the ashtray. He knocked it against the glass side, and the charred end fell into a pile of white powder.

"My grandfather was not a fighter pilot", I said.

"No", said Ursula.

"He flew an Avro Lancaster bomber."

"Yes", said Ursula.

"And in February of 1945, his plane was one of the planes that bombed Dresden."

"Yes."

"He never got over it, Ursula. Not until his dying day."

"No. Nor you, I think."

I raised my stained hands and dropped them. "My feelings are nothing in comparison. I don't believe in inherited guilt."

"And yet you feel guilty all the same", said Ursula. "Will you help us, Doctor McClelland?"

I said, "But I don't actually know who you are. If you are not BfV—"

"We are not BfV, but we are Germans. We are patriots."

Once again, the word made me wince, but my own little book, written in careful, scholarly German and thereby engraved into my memory, reproached me.

"What do you want me to do?" I asked.

"Very little", said Ursula. "We would like you to invite Suzy Davis to a late supper tonight at Il Gattopardo. Between nine and nine thirty. That is all."

"Why Il Gattopardo?"

"Because it is just on the other side of the Old Bridge. Miss Davis will cross there on her bicycle."

I hesitated. "What are you going to do to her?"

"We are going to talk to her."

"Yes, but what else?"

"You need not worry about that."

My eyes shifted away toward the sunny window. "I don't know. She's only a child, after all. A gullible child."

"A child? No." For the first time, the calm, grey sea of Ursula's demeanour was ruffled. "Suzy Davis is twenty-two, an adult. There were real children in the Hauptbahnhof. Both of them, here and in Dresden. You must have seen them yourself, Doctor McClelland. Children with schoolbags. Babies. And perhaps you saw pregnant women."

I said, "I need time to think."

"You have time but not too much. This is what we shall do. One of us will wait outside your building today. When you have invited Suzy Davis to dinner, open the windows. Understand?"

"She might be busy. There might be a party, some meeting ..."

"I think that she will accept your invitation", said Ursula. "She will want to clear the air."

"I am not comfortable with this", I said. "I do not know what I should do. I never wanted to get involved."

"*Tja*", said Ursula. "There was never any choice in the matter, Doctor McClelland. You are the European daughter of a European. You have always been involved."

* * *

I slipped a note under Suzy's door, asking her to visit me, and then I walked up to the Old Bridge where I caught a taxi to Bornheim. The streets were jammed, and I thought that perhaps Suzy would come by before I could get home. It depended, I supposed, on whether she had cancelled her rally or not. Certainly, bicycling was the fastest way to cross town that day.

Perhaps I wouldn't go home at all. I would go to the cinema and then have dinner by myself somewhere. The patriots would just have to come up with a new plan. But then I thought that I could try once more to convince Suzy to stop what she was doing and to go home to Toronto. So instead of going to the cinema, I went home and had a shower. The flat was very hot and stuffy. I opened a window in the sitting room—and then remembered that to this action there would be a reaction. There was a punk sitting across the street on a low wall, drinking a beer. An Alsatian in a spiked collar sat panting beside him. I shut the window again and went to the kitchen. I thought of eating, but there was nothing to eat. I thought of drinking, but there was the baby to consider. For the first time since the explosion, I thought about the baby. At the time, I did not realise that the explosion could have triggered a miscarriage. But as it didn't, it is just as well that I didn't have that to think of, too. The buzzer sounded, and I went to the intercom. But it was a man's voice that came through the box.

"Catriona, how is it going?"

"Marcus. What are you doing down there?"

Marcus was annoyed. "What am I doing? What am I always doing? Checking on you!"

"Thank you, Marcus. That is very kind. But I'm fine."

"Do you have enough food?"

"That's no longer a problem. The doctor cut my cast off."

"Are you going to let me in this time?"

"Not tonight, Marcus. But soon, I promise."

"Well, at least come downstairs so I can say that I saw you. Otherwise he's going to bite my arse."

"Who is?"

"Who do you think? Just come downstairs, okay?"

I went down the stairs and opened the door to the garden. Marcus stood there, goggling at me solemnly from under his Beatles cap.

"Dennis has been sending you to check up on me?"

"I can't say anything", said Marcus testily. "This is the stupidest business I have ever been mixed up in. But now at last I have seen you, and you are alive, and you look fine. Your hair looks good, by the way."

"Tell him that too. And tell him I'm dating a footballer. A big one. A pro."

"Whatever. This is stupid. It's hot out, and traffic is terrible. There was a bomb in the Hauptbahnhof, by the way. Twelve people died. One was only ten years old. Can't I come in for a beer?"

"No, Marcus, I'm sorry. But I'll get you one from the fridge."

I watched him walk, bottle in hand, across the street. As he passed the punk with the dog, the punk waved an empty can at him. Marcus dropped a coin or coins in the can, and the punk nodded his thanks. And before Marcus had walked out of sight, the buzzer sounded again.

"Hi, Cat!"

"Come in, Suzy."

She tramped up the stairs, swinging her bicycle helmet from the straps. "Thanks for inviting me over, Cat. I thought you were pissed off at me."

I led the way into the living room and sat down on the couch. Suzy followed me, taking sips of water from a squeeze bottle. She sat in Dennis' chair.

"I was pissed off", I said. "All those people, the children ..."

"Well, that wasn't my fault. It wasn't supposed to go off so soon. And believe me, I totally freaked at the guy who screwed up." She might have been telling me a story about a ticket agent who had misplaced her concert tickets. Still, it was enough to generate a hope.

"So have you washed your hands of him?"

"Well, I told him if he screwed up again, we'd be through with him."

"But shouldn't you be through with the rest of them, too?"

"No, of course not. They're my crew."

"Your what?"

"My peeps. My people."

"Suzy, couldn't you have ... ?" But I held my peace. There was no point.

"Couldn't have what?"

"Couldn't you have found a more pacific sect of Islam? The al-Mahdis, for example. And look at Aisha. Aisha believes in coexistence. Why don't you?"

"Aisha doesn't follow the purest form of Islam", said Suzy. "She is poorly taught at that mosque of hers. I kind of lost respect for her, you know? She's all talk, and no real action. Her attitude is more Turkish than Muslim. Islam isn't just one country. We're a people."

174

"The House of Peace", I said sourly.

"That's right", said Suzy. "But we want a just peace. And unfortunately, the only language the House of War understands is violence. So we have to act in self-defense."

"And so that was what the Hauptbahnhof bombings were. Self-defense." I got up and went to the windows. I threw one open. The punk was still sitting on the sidewalk with his dog. He had wires running out of his ears; he bobbed his head to some beat.

"Exactly", said Suzy. "I wasn't sure you'd understand."

"It's one political idea among many", I said. "Would you like to have supper with me tonight?"

"That would be great", said Suzy. "I'm totally stoked that you're not mad at me anymore, Cat."

I went into the study and opened the windows. I came back into the living room and opened the one window that remained closed. Then I sat down.

"Angry, no. Of course, I'm still shocked. It's a lot to absorb."

"I wish I could explain it as well as my imam", said Suzy wistfully. "You should meet him, Cat. He is a wonderful man. He's so funny, but he can be really serious, too. He's solid."

"Is he in Frankfurt?"

"No, he's . . .", Suzy wavered. "He's somewhere else. But there are other solid imams in Germany. There's a little mosque in Oberrad; they have a great outreach program."

"No thanks", I said. "Aisha lives in Oberrad. I avoid it on principle."

"Well, there's a fantastic one in Hamburg. It's really solid. They are on fire for the love of Islam, you know? The imam—he is so funny—he says he'll have to die on his feet because he won't rest until all Hamburg is safely in the Dar el Islam. But I guess Hamburg is a little far to go."

"A little", I said, and Suzy carried on about her favourite imams and books and mosques. I interrupted long enough to ask if she needed any more air, and she said she was fine. I got up and looked through the open window beside the couch. It had no screen. The punker was gone. Now an elderly man strolled up the street with a pedometer in his hand. I wondered which one was Ursula's watchman. Perhaps they both were. Had Ursula already heard the message of the open windows? If so, he was setting into motion his plan concerning Il Gattopardo and the Old Bridge. I couldn't imagine what it would be; the summer sunset was incredibly late in Frankfurt, and the banks of the Main would be dotted with tourists.

"Okay, I am totally talking your ears off", said Suzy. "But it's, like, a complete relief. I have all these thoughts buzzing around in my head, and I can't tell anybody. I have to act like a chameleon: with my Peace Now buddies, I can only talk the usual political stuff. And I don't really like talking girl stuff with my mosque friends. I can't even tell them about what I do for ... Well, anyway, I don't even have my crew to talk to because we communicate only through cell phones at prearranged times. But I feel like I can talk to you about everything. I don't know, maybe you think I'm boring, though."

"You're not boring", I said. "I'm just not in a chatty mood. Maybe I wouldn't be a good dinner companion tonight."

"Don't say that! We have to go. I've totally missed you. I feel like things have been different since ... Well ..."

"Since you took off with Dennis", I said.

"Well, no. I meant something else. Anyway, we had a great conversation that night in the village, eh? Sitting down in the basement, totally freaked out of our minds. But I think we shared something real, Cat. And I wish you'd come to the mosque and learn about Islam. But I also think, well, it's kind of cool that you're so nonjudgmental. I mean, even though the Nazis broke your leg, you never said anything bad about them. You're just so ... I don't know. Noncommittal."

"I might change", I said. "Sooner or later, we all do."

"But you haven't yet", said Suzy. "And being so open-minded means you're still open to truth. I doubt you'll change much—and neither will I. I'm totally committed to my path, you know?"

"You might change", I said. "Think about the Hauptbahnhof. Didn't that change your attitude a little?"

"Not really", said Suzy. "I've seen dead and injured people before. The only difference was that these people were white."

"Germans, Turks, and tourists. What if they had been Torontonians?"

"They wouldn't have been all white then", said Suzy, smiling. "Toronto is a totally multicultural city."

"But wouldn't you have felt a tremor of pain? Some would say that it is natural to feel more grief at the sufferings of those most like us. In racial makeup. In nationality."

"'Fighting was ordained for you, though you dislike it'", said Suzy, and it took me a moment to realise that she was quoting again. "'It may be that you dislike something that is good for you, and you like a thing that is bad for you. And Allah knows, but you do not know.' That's in the Koran."

"I suppose I should be able to counter with a dozen texts from the Bible", I said. "I think there's something in Jeremiah about natural law." But I was tired of the conversation. I wanted her to go away and be dealt with. Then I could start putting my life back together.

"You're hilarious", said Suzy. "Tell you what. Dennis has gone to meet Marcus somewhere. Why don't you and I go have coffee on the Zeil? Then we could do some shopping before dinner. What's the name of that place? We met there once, remember? With that lady from German *Vogue*?"

"I've been avoiding it, actually. Dennis and I used to go there all the time."

"Oh I'm sorry, Cat. I totally forgot. Well, why not somewhere nearby?"

"Can't do it, I'm afraid. I've got to go into the office now. It's on Kaiserstrasse, and God only knows what the U-Bahn is like tonight."

"That's too bad", said Suzy. "I was hoping for a girls' night out."

"I won't be able to get away until late", I said. "But I'll meet you halfway. Meet me at Il Gattopardo at nine. It's on my side of the Old Bridge."

"Okay. I guess I'll have to find something else to do until then." She sighed. "Maybe I'll go to a movie. Germans don't believe in subtitles, though, so almost everything from the States is dubbed."

"There should be at least one in English at Eschenheimer Turm."

"I've seen it already", said Suzie. She looked wistful and very young. I was suddenly assailed with the temptation to tell her everything, to get her out of Frankfurt if I had to drive her myself, to somehow get her on a plane back home to Toronto. But then she added, "I went with Dennis. He likes to practice his English whenever he can."

"There are all the museums down by the river", I said. "There's lots to see." And then, as my wavering conscience turned toward Suzy once again—"Or you could grab the train to Dreieich and see the ruined castle. If you got back too late for dinner, it wouldn't matter much. Come up afterward and see me here."

"I'd better not take a regional train", said Suzy. "They'll be watching the stations, and you never know."

177

"Whatever you like", I said. She had been given her chance, and I had made my choice. No going back on it now. "Anyway, don't expect me before nine. Now I'll have to say good-bye, Suzie. I want to send off some emails before I look in at the office."

"Cool", said Suzy gaily, getting up. "Catch you later!"

Her footsteps clattered down the stairs. The street door shut with a polite and muted bang. I sat on the couch for a long time, staring at the bookcases in the hall. Then I got up, fetched the vacuum cleaner out of the kitchen, and removed every physical trace of Suzy Davis from my home.

* * *

The trains were running on time again. I took the U-Bahn to Hauptwache and walked slowly toward Kaiserstrasse. The city centre was unusually quiet for six o'clock. It looked as if everyone had simply gone home early. Knots of teenagers stood around looking glum. The riots, if there were riots in Frankfurt, wouldn't begin until later, once the sun had set and the teenagers were good and drunk. The office, which I shared with a number of other bureaus, was noisy with activity. Behind glass partitions, journalists chatted into phones while typing.

"Where the hell have you been?" said George Santos, flashing his straight, white, American teeth. "This is your department, Religion Lady. We got a press release, and it's the Muzzies all right."

"Al-Q?"

"Al-Q Junior", said George. "Translated it comes out to 'Red Knights of the Quarter Moon', or some crap like that. Did you see the Hauptbahnhof?"

"I saw it."

"They made a hell of a mess. We got an ID on that kid who died. Get this: he wasn't even German. Pakistani. Muhammad Shamir Panju. Only Pakistani kid in his class. A Muzzie himself, of course. Frigging irony, huh?"

"It's very sad."

"They're thinking of imposing a curfew on kids in Berlin tonight."

"Jesus have mercy", I said. "Where did you hear that?"

"Simon Reinhardt. He's just on his way back from there. Think they'll do that here?"

"How would they enforce it?"

178

"Good point. Anyway, I'm off to call a man about a dog. Want to go out for a beer later?"

"I've got a dinner engagement at Il Gattopardo at nine."

"That's where I'm meeting Simon", said George. "Tell me when you leave, and I'll go with you."

I went into my glass cubicle and checked my emails again. The statement from the German bishops on the bombing had been released. I turned it into a sound bite and emailed it to New York. Then I got started on what I thought my editor would really like: a firsthand account of the bombing, with heavy emphasis on the dead child, Muhammad Shamir, and a melancholy reflection on religious violence. I left out Dennis, Suzy, and the unborn baby saved from an early death (perhaps) by a large crate of blackberries. I carefully stripped the scene of any violent emotion like longing, anger, or vengeance. I wrote in the still, sad music of humanity and ended on a coda of hope. It reminded me of the naïve, young, spiritual sentimentalist I was once upon a time. When it was done, I fetched George from his cubicle, and we walked to Il Gattopardo together. The dying sun burned against our backs.

The restaurant patio was dotted with European businessmen looking slightly uncomfortable, as if they had intruded on a family tragedy. But the restaurant itself was crammed with journalists, all as merry and hilarious as they had been after the Berlin bombing. The *Oberkellner* informed me that there would be a fifteen-minute wait for a table. I put my name down for a table for two and went to the bar with George. It was easy to pretend Suzy was really coming. I even jested to George about the perpetual lateness of my friend.

I stood to one side of the bar and sipped at a cranberry and soda, pretending to listen to George and his freckled pal from the *Frankfurter Allgemeine*. Instead, I looked around the restaurant at the unmistakable ladies and gentlemen of the press. Even those sitting alone entered into the convivial spirit of the evening by shouting into mobiles as they ate. Only one of them, a blonde woman sitting at a table near the door, appeared to be working. She frowned through chic reading glasses into her laptop computer. Her glasses and severe suit seemed to reproach the foreigners laughing all around her. She was a living symbol of German productivity. Perhaps she was criticising the rail system for not coping better with the delays arising from the bombing.

Petra Schattschneider came in with a charming young man who turned out to be her new boyfriend, and I ordered another cranberry and soda. I wanted to go on pretending that Suzy was really coming, and that would be more difficult once I sat down and began my pointless wait. Of course, there was a chance that she really would come. The best-laid schemes of mice and men aft gang agley. But I wasn't sure if I did want to see her come through the door. Berlin, Dresden, Frankfurt . . . Had Suzy inflicted any more damage on her host country since she had bicycled from my flat? It seemed quite likely. One could argue that she had been fighting her jihad on two fronts, one overt, one covert, ever since she arrived. But it seemed unlikely that Ursula would come up with a solution that did not also involve death. The thought made me queasy, and when the *Oberkellner* showed me to my table, I realised that in order to keep up my pretense I'd have to force myself to eat.

It was a quarter past nine. The sun had vanished under the skyscrapers, and the outdoor lights shone out. The murmuring businessmen outside my open window were cloaked in shadows thrown by the tiny candles on their tables. I hadn't thought to bring a book. All I had to distract myself was the menu and the antics of the other journalists. I ordered an antipasto plate, citing the lateness of my friend, and a third cranberry and soda. I stared into the night, past the patio toward the Old Bridge. Cars rumbled over it, and bicycles darted beside the sidewalks. I couldn't see as far as the other side. My ears strained to catch—what? A scream? A shot? A sudden splash? I spent a long time picking at the antipasto. The waitress began to hover. For her benefit alone, I called my late friend's mobile. Suzy didn't answer, and I rang off, heart pounding. Then I went ahead and ordered veal cutlets. It seemed appropriate to the occasion.

At the bar, Petra's young boyfriend put his arm around her tidy waist, and as I drank my fourth cranberry and soda, I thought, for the first time since Suzy left my flat, of Dennis. I remembered how Suzy, huddled up in the corner of the couch in the cellar, had said he seemed like a hero in a book, and I had called him, "Saint Dennis, patron saint of hair gel and clubbing". Which one of us had a better estimation of who he really was? And what would he say if Suzy didn't come back to the postmodern flat that night? Would he be shocked? Worried? Heartbroken? And for the thousandth time, I wondered what it was about Suzy that had attracted him in the first place.

Was it really her youth? Her charming naïveté? Her exotic foreignness? After two years of my silent pessimism, had Dennis turned to her passionate optimism with relief? I played once again the scene of our last and violent quarrel in my mind. "You'll be sorry", he had said. And I was sorry. Presumably, he was sorry too, as he had felt guilty enough to send Marcus to check up on me. Unless, of course, it hadn't been guilt. Unless, of course, the whole affair had been a way to make me realise what I was losing. Unless, of course, Dennis had seen in Suzy a way to make me knuckle under. Unless, of course, he was just using her.

I choked on my drink, and for a panicked moment I thought I would vomit over the table. When the nausea subsided, I looked at my watch. It was a quarter to ten. I might be too late to save her. But on the other hand, I might not. I waved over the waitress and explained rapidly that my friend might be wandering in the street, having forgotten the address. As I explained, I pressed a sheaf of euros into her hand and got up from the table. I must have looked quite ill; the chattering diners glanced up as I made my way past their tables. And the severe blonde woman near the door actually caught my arm as I passed her.

"Doctor McClelland", she said in English. "You are Doctor McClelland?"

I knew that voice. I looked into the woman's face, and Dennis' blue eyes, strangely fringed with blonde lashes, stared into mine. She was Aisha. My heart thudded to a painful stop, and I forgot all about Suzy. I had never before seen Aisha's hair. It was pulled into a ponytail away from her face, and it spilled down her blue, tailored back. Her pencil skirt was well above her knees. She was wearing pantyhose and high-heeled shoes.

"You are Catriona McClelland?" asked Aisha, and her eyes held a warning.

"Yes", I stammered. "Yes, I am Catriona McClelland."

"I'm very happy to meet you", said Aisha grimly, and she pulled a slim volume from the shoulder bag hanging from her chair. "I would be gratified if you would sign your book for me."

I stared at her as she offered me a pen. She leaned forward.

"Sit down", she hissed in German.

Dazed, I sat down and took her pen.

"And to whom should I address it?" I asked in English, not without irony.

"To a patriot", said Aisha, and I knew Suzy was already dead.

Head swimming, I opened the book to the title page and looked at the blankness under the title. At last, I began to write.

Aisha got up and stood behind me, pretending to be interested in what I was writing. She leaned over and murmured in my ear, "Ursula thought you might compromise your alibi. You can't leave yet."

"So you're a patriot", I muttered back. "Your grandfather thought he was a patriot, too."

"We all have grandfathers", said Aisha. "I'm in this for my grandchildren. And for your grandchildren also."

"Grandchildren. What about your brother? Is he a patriot too? Or did you just use him as bait?"

Aisha went back to her chair and took a package of cigarettes from her bag. She offered me one. I reached forward, and then remembered the baby. I shook my head.

"It wasn't supposed to go that far", said Aisha. She spoke in a low tone, and I had to lean forward to hear her. All around us the journalists laughed and chatted. "To be frank, I didn't think you would ever let him leave you."

"Well, you were wrong about that", I said. "He left me all right."

"It was a most unpleasant shock, I admit", said Aisha. "It made things much more difficult and dangerous for me."

"For you? Why for you? For her, you mean."

Aisha ignored this. "Dennis, of course, knows nothing about tonight. But there are those who might wonder. I want you to take him out of the country."

"How can I? He left me."

Aisha sat silently and smoked, deliberating the question.

"I think he'll be back", she said at last. "I am not sure, but it seems to me likely. And if he does come back, I want you to take him away as soon as you can. Not to Scotland. To Canada. Toronto, if you like. Just for two months or so. Can you do that?"

"I could do it—if he agreed. But I have a new job starting in December. In Rome."

"That doesn't matter", said Aisha. She leaned back, and a look of relief flickered over her stony face. "Rome is better than here."

"He doesn't know about you either, does he?"

"Nobody at home knows about me", said Aisha.

"Not even Tarkan?"

"Tarkan", said Aisha, with a cold smile. "Especially not Tarkan. But now you do, Catriona. It's ironic, isn't it? I know very well how much you hate me."

"I don't hate you, H–Hannah." My breath rasped over her Christian name. "I didn't understand . . . I didn't appreciate . . ."

"Whatever", she said. "We're too alike to ever be friends, Citizen *Keine*. But you love my brother, don't you?"

"Yes. Yes, better than I knew."

"That is good", said Aisha. "Call Suzy's phone again." She stood up and said, in a slightly louder voice, "I must go now to my appointment, but I appreciate very much you speaking with me. I look forward to reading more of your thoughts on Germany."

"You're very welcome", I said. We shook hands, and I went into the ladies' restroom. When I came out, she was gone. I went back to my table and ordered a cup of tea. The waitress was solicitous. "You couldn't find your friend?"

"I've completely given her up", I said.

When I finished my tea, I paid the bill and said a few words to my acquaintances at the bar. It was a quarter past ten when I left Il Gattopardo. The night was clear and fine and terribly hot. Hesitating for a moment, I crossed over the Old Bridge into Sachsenhausen. The bars and restaurants along Elisabethenstrasse were emptier than usual, but their lights and music still streamed into the street. I walked near the tourist tavern without glancing at it and turned right at Textorstrasse. I wasn't sure which window was Suzy's, so I didn't look up at her building to see if her lights were on or not. I turned at Brückenstrasse and made straight across the square for the Südbahnhof. I took an S-train to Konstablerwache and transferred to my U-train. Then I got off and walked to my flat house. The air was heavy with the scent of dying roses. I opened the door to the stairwell, and I knew at once that Dennis was above.

Chapter 3

Class had let out half an hour before. Dennis dropped his messenger bag in the hallway with a thump.

"Hallo", he called. "Where are you?"

I said, "On the couch." It was still hot; I didn't feel like moving.

"Did the Kommissar come by?"

"Yes, but he's gone now. He won't be back."

Dennis scraped off his sandals and padded down the hall. He eyed the piece of paper in my hands.

"What's that?"

"An offer from a London publisher. They want me to translate my little book for them."

"So. You will reveal all our secrets to our British cousins. Just great, I'm living with a spy. How much?"

"Thousands and thousands of euros, apparently. My agent is drinking champagne."

"Excellent", said Dennis. He collapsed on the couch and settled his head in my lap. "So when are we getting married?"

"Join the queue. I had a footballer after me, you know."

"*Quatsch.* Footballers. You'd be bored senseless. Footballers have no brains."

"But think of my self-confidence. If I could pull a footballer, I could probably keep some poor philosophy student tied to me for life."

"Probably", said Dennis. "So when *are* we getting married?"

I looked down at his impudent face. His eyes held a renewed challenge; I met it head on. "Monday, if we can get an appointment."

"Are you serious?"

"Very serious."

He narrowed his suddenly suspicious eyes. "And a church wedding?"

"Next weekend, if Uncle Franz permits."

"Next weekend? My mother will have a heart attack", said Dennis. "What changed your mind?"

"Life and death. Sins of commission and omission. Self-knowledge and repentance. Ten horrible minutes in the Südbahnhof when I thought you were there."

"Is it also because I went away?"

Was it my imagination, or did I now read guilt in those blue irises?

"Partly. It gave me time to think."

"Ah. So you thought. And did you conclude finally that I am not a little child?"

"You can't be a little child", I said. "You're going to be a father."

Dennis shifted his head to my knee, so as to look directly into my face. "What do you mean?"

"Exactly what I said."

"Unbelievable. When?"

"March."

"If a baby is coming in March, then I am already a father. When did it happen?"

"Eight weeks ago. Maybe nine."

"*Mein Gott*. Why didn't you tell me?"

"I just found out myself. I had the first ultrasound yesterday. Get up. I have pictures."

I took the photographs out of my bag and showed him.

Dennis said, "He looks like an alien from outer space."

"They always do at the beginning."

He jumped up from the couch. "I have to call my mother. This is unbelievable."

"Will she be cross, do you think?"

"Are you joking? It will be Christmas and Easter on the same day for my mother. Uncle Franz will launch a thunderstorm at us, but it doesn't matter. He'll do the ceremony when we want. It won't be the first bon-bon wedding in the family. Hannah came early too, did you know?"

"No."

"They hushed the whole thing up. Mum and Dad always celebrate their wedding anniversary two months earlier. They think we don't know. You know how they are."

He went into the office, and I heard him say, "Hallo, Mutti? Yes, Mutti, I have some good news. But—ah—I think you should sit down. Well, I will tell you why. Just sit down, please."

I took the gold chain from around my neck and slid both my gold engagement ring and the aluminum Miraculous Medal into my hand. I pushed the ring onto my fourth finger with a little difficulty. Either the heat or pregnancy had made my hands swell a little. I put the Miraculous Medal back on the chain. For some reason, it made me think of Suzy. There had been no miracle for Suzy.

From the office came a small and tinny scream and a torrent of high-pitched words. Dennis appeared in the doorway with the phone held away from his ear, grimacing. I grimaced back.

"But we don't want a big party, Mutti. Just make a reservation at *Zum Linzer* . . . It doesn't matter . . . It doesn't *matter* . . . Well, then make a reservation somewhere else . . . Wait a minute, please." He covered the receiver with his hand. "And just where do you think you're going?"

"Into the garden. I want to deadhead the roses before it rains."

"You're not leaving me alone with my mother. Hallo, Mutti? Mutti, I have to go. I want to call Uncle Franz. No, *I* will call Uncle Franz. Naturally, I am going to tell him about the baby . . . Well, if he knows about the baby, he won't make any objections, will he . . . ? Yes, but he'll *know* we're not getting married just because of the baby . . . No, of course, we aren't. Haven't we been together for years? That doesn't count. That was nothing. A misunderstanding. *Klar.* You want me to ask her? I'll ask her." He turned his face from the phone. "Are we getting married just because of the baby?"

"No", I said. "We're getting married because we're adults, I love you, and I can't live without you."

"There", said Dennis to his mother. "We're adults, she loves me, and she can't live without me . . . I don't know why either. She's insane, perhaps. Unbelievable. I'm having a baby with a crazy woman."

I took a knife from the kitchen and went downstairs. The August roses bobbed their heads in the slight breeze. The white ones had had it, but a few great red-and-yellow blooms still blossomed in the dark green hedges. I set to work severing droopy or faded heads, so that the plants could concentrate on producing new ones. From the kitchen came the sound of the fridge opening and shutting, and Dennis remonstrating with his uncle over the phone. I thought of Suzy staring wistfully out the kitchen window at the lilac bushes, long since blown. She had been homesick, and now it was I who would be going to our shared birthplace with the man we both loved. Now that she was dead, I had everything I could want. Everything . . . except a clear conscience.

The door slammed, and Dennis came outside with a bottle of beer. He grinned and wiped his forehead.

"Well, that's done", he said. "There's just one little thing, though. Uncle Franz says we have to go to confession right before. Don't make that face. It won't kill you to go to confession—even to Uncle Franz."

"I hate going to confession", I said. "Uncle Franz will expect me to say I'm sorry for things I'm not sorry for, and I don't want to tell him the things I am sorry for. The words will stick in my throat. They'll choke me."

"You could write a list", said Dennis. "That's what I do."

"A list. I might as well write a book. *Confessions of Catriona McClelland*. Dedicated to His Eminence Franz Cardinal Kessler."

"Don't do that", said Dennis. "Just write a list."

The late-afternoon sun shone on the bushes. Dennis sat on the doorstep to watch me work. I felt reluctant to break the peace that had sprung up between us. But there was something I had to ask.

"Dennis, do you . . . miss . . . Suzy?"

His eyes darted away, and he began to fiddle with a disembodied blossom.

"Not exactly", he said. "Miss. No. But I'm sorry."

"Sorry for what?"

"Just sorry."

"I'm sorry, too."

The memory of Herr Krause, the kindly policeman, rose before me, flipping through the *Catechism* with something akin to priestly authority. "Legitimate public authority". And yet I had taken the cab from the Südbahnhof not to the police station but to Ursula. No, I was not the kind of woman to hold another woman's head under water until she drowns. But I was the kind of woman who would stand by and let it happen if it made life more pleasant for me. Through my fault, through my fault, through my grievous fault.

"*Ach*", said Dennis, breaking into my thoughts. "You. You did nothing to be sorry for. You were a better friend than I was. I shouldn't have . . . Well . . . I just shouldn't have."

"I understand", I said. "You can save it for Uncle Franz."

Our Catholic faith teaches that the slightest movement of repentance, even at the very moment of death, is enough to welcome the forgiveness of God. I wondered if Suzy, confronted by whoever waited for her by the Old Bridge, had been allowed the opportunity for regret. Dennis was sorry. I was sorry. I hoped Suzy had been sorry, too. She should have been allowed at least that; I wouldn't have wanted her to have left with nothing.

ACKNOWLEDGMENTS

Fellow devotees will have perceived my debt to Graham Greene's *The Quiet American*. Explicit thanks go to Nancy Cummings and Tricia Postle, who read each chapter as soon as I wrote it, and to Mark McLean for keeping a Scots eye on Catriona's diction. Thanks also to Volker Meitner, Daniel Santoro, and Bartosz Gradecki for their suggestions and to Michael Cummings for explaining the workings of fan belts. I am very grateful to Richard Greene; Father Gilles Mongeau, SJ; Father John Emerson, FSSP; and Olga and Brent McAdam for their cheerful encouragement.